W0006441

THE
Light-Fingered Gang

DAVE GLAZE

COTEAU
BOOKS
FOR KIDS

This novel is a work of fiction. Names, characters, places, and incidents either are the product of the author's imagination or are used fictitiously. Any resemblance to actual persons, living or dead, is coincidental.

Edited by Barbara Sapergia.
Cover images: *model*: Denique LeBlanc; *photographer*: Paul Austring; *background*: "Downtown Saskatoon, c.1912," courtesy, Saskatoon Public Library.
Cover montage and design by Duncan Campbell.
Book design by Duncan Campbell and Karen Steadman.
Printed and bound in Canada by Gauvin Press.

Library and Archives Canada Cataloguing in Publication

Glaze, Dave, 1947—
The light-fingered gang / Dave Glaze.

(1912: The Mackenzie Davis files ; 1)
ISBN 1-55050-326-X

1. Saskatoon (Sask.)—Juvenile fiction. I. Title. II. Series.
PS8563.L386L53 2005   jC813'.54   C2005-904903-0

10 9 8 7 6 5 4 3 2 1

2517 Victoria Ave.
Regina, Saskatchewan
Canada S4P 0T2

Available in Canada & the US from
Fitzhenry & Whiteside
195 Allstate Parkway
Markham, ON, L3R 4T8

The publisher gratefully acknowledges the financial support of its publishing program by: the Saskatchewan Arts Board, the Canada Council for the Arts, the Government of Canada through the Book Publishing Industry Development Program (BPIDP), and the City of Regina Arts Commission.

To Verne Clemence (1937–2004),
a friend to all writers.

The Daily Phoenix

MONDAY, JANUARY 1, 1912

UNEQUALLED RIVER LOCATION CAUSE FOR CITY'S GROWTH

Demand For Construction Cannot Keep Pace

The remarkable growth of Saskatoon from a hamlet of 113 people in 1901 to 18,096 in 1911 is unequalled in the history of Canada. The percentage of increase in Saskatoon is so absurdly large as to make it scarcely worth quoting.

These years have seen the opening of vast areas of land all across Saskatchewan for the planting of hard wheat and Saskatoon, situated on the banks of the South Saskatchewan River, was the natural centre. The three railway systems saw it at once and fixed upon Saskatoon as a meeting place for railways and trade. At the present time the Wonder City of the West has more trains coming in and going out every day than any other city in Saskatchewan and the number will only increase in the future.

The year 1911 has eclipsed all former years in the number of houses and buildings erected so that a view from Caswell Hill now presents an impressive look to the visitor. The only embarrassment, and a temporary one it is, remains the difficulty for men and machines to keep pace with the demand for the construction of not just the buildings but the proper paved streets, concrete sidewalks, and water and sewage lines rightly expected by citizens of such a metropolitan city as ours. The year 1912 promises to see tremendous strides being made to remedy these understandable shortcomings.

CHAPTER ONE
Friday, July 9, 1912

I'm stuck

MACKENZIE DREW HIS FINGERS OVER THE warm, gnarled ridges of the building's freshly-cut stone blocks. He stepped away from the wall and rubbed the dust from his hands over the front of his white shirt. Peering into a window, he gently tugged the peak of his new tan-coloured cap. He twisted a little to the left, and to the right, and smiled at his reflection. He turned and followed the wooden sidewalk that passed under the awning of Harry Tupling's Men's Furnishings and beside a yard of yellow grass baking in the sun. Further down the street he spied his friend Albert on the steps to his father's office. "ABC Land Sales," read a newly painted sign on the side of the building. "Albert B. Crawley, Sr., Prop."

Mackenzie halted. A few inches from his feet, a grasshopper squatted on the boardwalk. Hunching its back, the creature crackled its dry, dusty wings. Mackenzie slid his scuffed boot forward until the insect sprang onto his pant leg. Keeping an eye on the grasshopper, he walked stiff-legged down the sidewalk to where Albert leaned back against the front of the white clapboard building, his eyes closed. Mackenzie slid his hand down his pant leg and scooped the insect into his palm.

"It was a day like this," he said, "that made the great Canadian runner Tom Longboat collapse from the heat. The Chicago Marathon. July 6, 1909."

"A little heat never stops Johnny Hayes," Albert said, without opening his eyes. "Marathons or ten-milers. America's Johnny Hayes keeps running."

"Longboat's the fastest man ever," Mackenzie said. "But he's a big man. The heat's probably harder on him than someone who's only five feet tall."

"Five feet four inches." Albert held up four fingers. "Tall enough to win in Chicago."

"All right." Mackenzie said. "Here, I got you a prize." When Albert opened his eyes, Mackenzie pressed the grasshopper into his hand. Albert peeked at the insect through a crack between his curled fingers.

"Shoot! He got me." Smearing the brown juice on the leg of his short pants, Albert grumbled, "We could have something better than this in our hands. We could have gold, money, jewels. Enough to make us rich. You can't keep telling me you're not interested."

2

"Why do you think there's all that precious stuff down there?"

"Because, you lunkhead," Albert said, "people are always dropping things and they don't even know it. When I lived in Minneapolis, Minnesota, I found scads of money under the boardwalks." Pushing himself onto his feet, Albert stood a head shorter than his friend. "Come on," he said.

The boys headed back toward Harry Tupling's – "The Nifty Man's Store" according to a sign on the awning. Albert stopped by a little gully that dipped under the boardwalk.

"This is made for us," he said. "There's lots of room to crawl under. We'll find good things for sure. We split everything fifty-fifty, right? It doesn't matter who sees it first. Partners. Shake?"

Mackenzie stepped into the hollow and dropped to his knees, then onto all fours. "Are you sure?" he asked, peering under the boards. He took off his cap and set it like a golden crown on a bush of spindly weeds.

"Where did you get that lid?" Albert asked.

"My mother ordered it from the Hudson's Bay Company catalogue. It's for good. I can't let it get dirty."

"It should be safe there. Hurry up, will you. You're being a slow Stanley."

Stretching out onto his belly, Mackenzie muttered, "I'm just taking a look."

The sidewalk's six-foot planks were nailed on top of pieces of wood that kept them a few inches off the ground and made a bridge over the gully. Mackenzie caterpillared under the boardwalk and into a wallow of powdery, dried-up mud. Gulping a mouthful of dust, he hawked and spit. Before he could back out, Albert kicked the soles of his boots.

"Move over," he said, "so I can get in."

Mackenzie put his arms across his chest and log-rolled toward Harry Tupling's. After a couple of turns his body jammed face-up into the boards above him. "Hey!" he called. "I'm stuck."

From the corner of his eye, Mackenzie saw Albert pull himself into the hole, turn, then squirm like a seal away from him. He felt like he was trapped inside a wooden box. The air was hot and stale, like in an attic on a summer day. Dust sparkled in the shafts of sunlight falling between the planks and tickled his throat. A picture came into his mind of a small boy who lay like this, hands clasped over his chest and eyes lightly closed. His little wooden box was lined with puffy purple cloth and set on a table. The people who walked by to gaze down at the boy were crying.

The sound of footsteps approached on the board-walk above. Two women stopped nearby and talked about the price of men's tweed trousers and vests. With a swish of dresses, they walked to the door of Harry Tupling's and entered.

"Albert!" Mackenzie cried. "I'm getting out."

SITTING ON THE EDGE of the boardwalk a few minutes later, Albert looked up at Mackenzie. "What happened to you?" he asked.

"I was stuck. I couldn't go anywhere." Mackenzie beat the flat of his hand over his chest and legs. "Do my back. What did you find?"

Albert got up and patted Mackenzie, once on each shoulder. "Nothing," he said. "But I didn't get very far." He rubbed a grey smudge on his shirt. "Next time you can try where I was. There's lots of room."

A voice shrieked across the street. "One dirty piggy! Two dirty piggies!"

On the far boardwalk, two girls clasped hands and doubled over giggling. Eunice McMahon wore a red-and-white dress with a matching red shopping bag slung from her elbow. "Piggy-wiggy-wiggy!" she called, straightening up. Dressed in pink, Ruth Anne Hardcastle pushed up her spectacles and patted her bonnet in place.

"How long have they been there?" Mackenzie asked.

"Badger Breath!" Albert shouted. "You have five seconds to get out of my sight." Bending down, he picked up a small rock and held it over his head so the girls could see it. "You too, Four Eyes."

Standing near one of the large windows in front of McMahon's Dry Goods store, Eunice screwed up her face like she'd just stepped on a fresh road apple. Mackenzie knew that look well. The two girls were in the same classroom with him and Albert in Victoria School. The girls' families had been living in Saskatoon for six years and they acted like anyone new to the school was too dirty and stupid to belong. About two weeks after Albert had moved from Minneapolis, Eunice and Ruth Anne had tattled on him for carving his initials into a desk. The principal, Mr. Millburn, had given Albert the strap.

Albert wound up and fired his rock. The girls screamed and rushed to the door. Like the bullet of a wild west gunfighter, the stone whacked into the wooden siding a few inches below the window.

"Skedaddle, you ugly varmints!" Albert cried.

Mackenzie backed into the lot. "She'll get her father after you," he said before sprinting toward the alley. Peering over his shoulder, he saw Albert pick up another stone, toss it in his palm, and walk toward the ABC office.

Clattering typewriter keys

JUST INSIDE THE DOOR TO *The Daily Phoenix*, Mackenzie stopped and took a deep breath. Ink. Machinery oil. Paper fresh from the mill. He breathed again. Cigar smoke. Even blindfolded, he would know he was in a newspaper office.

In three steps Mackenzie was at the counter that ran across the front of the room. His father, Theodore

Davis, sat bent over a typewriter at a desk on the far side. His fingers fell on the clattering typewriter keys, paused, then struck again. A moment later his hands rose and hovered over the letters, his eyes fixed on the words that had just appeared on the yellow paper curled above the machine.

Behind Mackenzie's father a door with a window of rippled glass opened to the office of Mr. Aikin. Mackenzie spied the editor hunched over his immense desk, shouting into the mouthpiece of the newspaper's telephone. Blue smoke from a cigar coiled around the receiver the man held like a fragile cup close to his ear. Mr. Aikin was in shirt sleeves, his jacket hanging from the knob of the office's safe.

A second door in the back wall was closed. Sometimes Mackenzie's father took him through that door to the composing room. There, sitting on a steel stool, a typesetter operated the linotype machine that noisily prepared the lines of words that would be printed in the newspaper.

Near the end of the counter, a wrought-iron wicket, like a teller's cage at a bank, surrounded Miss Price. A man leaned over the counter, his nose almost touching the grill. Mackenzie shuffled closer.

"Have you got that?" the man asked, pulling on the ends of his moustache. "I'm paying for each word, so I don't want any mistakes."

Miss Price said something that Mackenzie couldn't hear.

"All right," the man said and read from a piece of paper he held in front of him. *"For sale. Snap! Large rooming house having 22 rooms. Each big enough to comfortably hold two men with lots to spare."* He looked up. "If you put in double bunks, they'll take four men, maybe more. But if I say that, Doc McKay will have his snoops out trying to find some reason to outlaw it. Anyone with an eye for real estate will know what I mean."

He checked his paper again. "Okay, then it says, *Well located. Pleasantly finished. Sewer and water lines nearby. Easily made modern."* Peering at Miss Price, he added, "Some of the people you get in these rooming houses, they don't even want city water. They're not used to it where they come from. They're happy enough without it."

The man ran his finger down the paper. "Then, *Price, $14,500. Half cash, balance arranged. See the House Man, 102 Cahill Block."* He folded the paper. "That's me. The House Man. Now, how much will that cost?"

As she answered, Miss Price drew a white handkerchief from the sleeve of her dress, touched it to the tip of her nose, then slipped it back into her sleeve. The man acted surprised. "That much?" he said. "The *Star's* being much more considerate."

Mackenzie headed back toward his father but stopped to glance at a copy of the *Daily Phoenix* morning paper lying on the counter.

AMUSING AUTO ACCIDENT

Store Window Lost to Motor Car Reversal
Operator Denies Error, Demands Full Investigation

Smiling at the headline, Mackenzie read on:

An accident that had its amusing side took place shortly after noon yesterday when Mr. Geary of Geary and Smithwick was cranking his Studebaker Touring Car. Like many automobilists, Mr. Geary had reversed his motor car against the curb when parking some time earlier. Apparently the automobile was not left in neutral but rather in the reversing gear with the result that as soon as Mr. Geary began to turn the crank the car started to back. Although Mr. Geary pulled on the crank with might and main he was ruthlessly hauled over the sidewalk by the car which crashed its rear into the plate glass window of the Adilman and Adilman general store. It was only last month that a similar fate befell another automobile and a different window.

Mr. Geary, an automobilist with two years experience, has told police investigators that he is certain that he left his motor car in neutral and with the brake engaged. Charging that his vehicle was tampered with, Mr. Geary has recommended in the strongest language that police increase their vigilance against the criminal element who prey on automobiles and their operators.

When Mackenzie looked up, his father spotted him and raised one hand. He rolled the yellow paper partly out of his typewriter, nodded, then yanked it free and slapped it down on his desk. Pulling a pencil from behind his ear, he wrote a few words, then spun round to face Mackenzie.

"Hello, son," he said, wrinkling the skin around his eyes into what Mackenzie's mother called laugh lines. "Do you have the list?"

"Yes. Right here." Mackenzie patted his pants pocket.

Pushing his wheeled chair away from the desk, his father stood up. He wore a low-collared white shirt, the sleeves pulled back onto his forearms and held in place by a pair of black elastic arm bands. Lifting his jacket from a coat stand, he dropped a pencil and a black notebook into one pocket. He put on his straw boater and lightly tapped the top. When he reached the counter, he raised a section that lifted on hinges, and stepped through to join Mackenzie.

"I'll be back in thirty minutes!" he called.

Miss Price glanced at the clock on the wall beside her, then nodded at the woman approaching her wicket.

On their way down Twentieth Street, Mackenzie's father asked, "Is that dirt all over your clothes?" He swatted his son's chest with his open hand. "It is. Turn around. You can't go about looking like that. Your mother would be horrified. She works hard to keep you in clean clothes." He beat his palm over Mackenzie's back.

Mackenzie pulled a folded paper from his pocket and held it out.

Skimming his eyes down the page, his father read, "One tin Libby's corned beef, half a dozen lemons, quarter pound Keen's mustard powder, eight-ounce tin Royal baking powder, one spool white thread. I can't buy all this. I have all of four bits to my name." He shook his head. "We'll go to the Cairns Store and see what we can do." Mackenzie followed his father around the corner onto Second Avenue.

"Was that your story about Mr. Geary's motor car?" he asked.

"Yes. Did you like it? What a mess there was! Poor Mr. Geary really thinks that someone moved the gears on his automobile."

"You don't?"

"No. Why would anyone go to the bother? I think he's just being a bit forgetful. Or maybe he doesn't want to admit the damage those machines can do." He gripped Mackenzie's arm. "Whoa," he said. "Here's someone else who could do a bit of damage."

A dark green motor car roared toward them down the middle of the street. Fitted with goggles and a leather cap fastened under his jaw, the driver stared straight ahead. A voice cried out as a wagon lurched into the intersection. A woman on the wagon's seat clutched two young children to her chest. The teamster was on his feet calling to his two horses and pulling hard on their reins. Knocking against each other, the horses staggered to a stop.

The automobilist wrenched his steering wheel. The motor car slid toward the terrified horses, its front wheels ploughing through loose dirt. Everyone watching froze until the wheels suddenly gripped a patch of hard ground and the car veered away. With a quick look at the frightened family, the driver sped off.

Mackenzie's father released his hand. "That fool must have been driving at least twenty miles per hour," he said. Then he turned to the man who had stopped beside them. "Hello, doctor."

"They think they've turned into gods," Dr. McKay said, "They can move so fast, they don't have to act like humans anymore." Dr. McKay had a neat, dark beard and grey eyes that glinted, Mackenzie thought, like the steelies he and Albert played for in marbles.

Beside them, the horses whinnied and stepped back as the car's dust settled over them. Quietly slapping the reins over the horses' backs, the driver guided them across the street.

"I need to talk to you, Ted," Dr. McKay said. "It's typhoid season again. We have to tell people how to take care of themselves."

"Of course." Mackenzie's father pulled his notebook from his pocket.

"Not here," Dr. McKay waved his hand. "We'll sit down together so I can think about all I have to say." He pulled a watch by its chain from his jacket pocket and clicked open the cover. "I'm on my way to the Royal Hotel. My inspector tells me their restaurant is an awful mess." He snapped his watch closed. "Why don't you come along? You'll want to report on some of these eating places."

"What's the problem with the Royal? I've dined there."

Dr. McKay fixed Mackenzie's father in his gaze. "You might want to change that in the future," he said. "They use a basement room to store their supplies and prepare meals. It's a dirt-walled cellar that floods every time it rains. Even when the floor dries, the place is damp and mildewed."

"You don't say. Maybe I should take a look."

"Good," Dr. McKay said. "And afterwards we can talk about typhoid fever."

"Mackenzie, go let your mother know what's happened. Tell her I'll buy those articles later, perhaps tomorrow."

"May I come with you?"

His father hesitated.

"No," Dr. McKay said, looking over Mackenzie's head. "I don't think that would be a wise idea. It's not the sort of place you'd want a boy to spend much time in. Anything you touch is likely to be a breeding ground for germs."

"I'd be careful."

"You heard what Dr. McKay said." Mackenzie's father set his hand on his shoulder. "Hustle along. There will be things you can help your mother with."

The two men turned down the sidewalk. "The nasty thing about typhoid, Ted," Mackenzie heard the doctor say, "is that it's hardest on the babies."

Slowly Mackenzie started for home, feeling sorry that he was missing his father's investigation. Probably he would write a story about typhoid fever for tomorrow's *Phoenix*. The memory of the little boy came back to him. It was typhoid, he knew, that had put the young lad in his casket.

The hissing and chuffing of a steam engine

THE FOUR-YEAR-OLD TRAFFIC BRIDGE spanned the South Saskatchewan River from downtown to the east side of Saskatoon. The bridge's criss-crossing steel girders looked like a long black skeleton held aloft by the three concrete towers rising from the water. At the east end of the bridge, a road went straight up the steep riverbank called the Short Hill. Another street turned sharply to the left and took two blocks to climb the Long Hill. A third branch dipped down and followed the shoreline south.

Dr. McKay's house stood alone partway up the Short Hill. Its front steps and wide verandah faced the newly built Collegiate Institute whose massive weight seemed to have sunk the lowest of its four floors deep into the riverbank.

The hissing and chuffing of a steam engine greeted Mackenzie when he reached Victoria Avenue at the top of the Short Hill. The engine powered a trencher that scraped buckets of dirt from the ground to dig a long, straight trench.

Two dozen men wearing soft hats with wide, floppy brims and blue or grey coveralls over pale-coloured shirts swarmed around the machines. One crew fed coal from a wagon to the steam engine's boiler. Another ran the trencher. More men worked shoulder-deep in the ground, swinging picks and shovels to deepen the ditch. Others braced heavy boards against the sides of the completed trench. As they worked they called out to each other in the language people called Galician.

Near the workers stood three men dressed in homburgs, black suits, white shirts, and ties. Occasionally one of these men stepped closer to the machines or the trench and yelled an order. "Watch the pressure in the boiler!" "Don't waste that coal!" "Smooth out the bottom down there!" "Take an axe to that tree root!"

Outside the new Douglas Hardware, Mackenzie slowed down. Sheets of grey tin covered the walls of the building. Mackenzie reached out to touch the stone-like bulges that the tin had been shaped into. As he passed the screen door, he caught the oily steel smell of new tools. Glancing through the fine mesh, he could make out a pyramid of stacked paint cans. A man in a white shirt, a string tie, and a long apron strode out of the darkness. Mackenzie stepped back as the door swung open.

The man walked to the corner of the building where two other men sat facing each other on upturned barrels. One of them fed five strands of brown twine into a machine operated by the second. As he turned a crank, the strands were pulled into one end of the machine and came out the other as tightly braided rope that fell into a coil on the ground.

"How's that working?" asked the man in the apron.

"Smooth as silk, Mr. Douglas," the machine operator answered. "She's going to beat the band."

"That's probably enough for now," the owner said. "I need a hand getting a few cases of tinware downstairs."

"Yes, sir." The other man sprang up. Brushing against Mackenzie, he followed the owner into the store.

We never have enough

NELLIE SAT BY THE BACK STOOP, slapping baby-sized brown puffs in the powdered dirt. Above her, a row of white diapers were pinned like a ship's flags to a clothes line. Spotting her brother, Nellie squealed, rolled onto her feet, and took a step. "Mack! Mack!" she cried.

Mackenzie's mother eyed him from the top step. The skirt of her well-worn dress was hiked up to her knees. Between her legs a rusty pail held strips of potato skins. One step down, three peeled potatoes sat in a cooking pot.

"What have you been up to?" she asked, tucking a dark brown strand of hair into her neat bun. "You look like you've been rolling in the dirt."

Brushing his sleeves, Mackenzie said, "No. Maybe I leaned against something. I'm sorry."

"And what have you done with my shopping?"

Mackenzie scooped up Nellie and tapped his fingers against her ribs. His sister squealed, flailing her arms and legs. "I tried," he said. "Father didn't have much money, but we were going to go to Cairns anyway. Then we met Dr. McKay and father went with him to inspect the Royal Hotel restaurant."

"But Cairns is closed," Mackenzie's mother said, shaking her head, "from the fire. The *Phoenix* has been full of advertisements telling people to wait for their reopening. You'd think your father could remember something like that."

"Mack!"

Mackenzie swung his sister in front of his chest. She reached up, snatched his cap and held it over her head.

"I'll tickle you," Mackenzie said, poking his thumb into her armpit, and getting a huge yowl in return.

"Be careful with her, Mackenzie," his mother said. "And before you change your clothes, I'd like you to go ask Mrs. Bailey if she can spare us two pails of water."

"Again? It seems like we never have enough."

"Well, we don't," his mother said, her voice rising. "And we won't until we get clean water coming in those pipes we hear so much about. Now, do as you're told."

"Yes, Mother." Scowling, Mackenzie softly butted his head into Nellie's chest. When she cried out,

Mackenzie set her on the ground. Nellie studied her brother's new cap, then crumpled it into her face.

MACKENZIE TROD CAREFULLY down the rutted alley. With each step, water slopped up to the rims of the pails weighing down his arms.

Mr. Arnold's buggy, with Rose in harness, turned into the far end of the lane. As Mr. Arnold waved from his seat, Rose steered herself off the alley and into her stable across from Mackenzie's house. The man climbed down from the buggy. Talking quietly to his horse, he began to unfasten the harness.

Mackenzie set down his load and shook his arms. After brushing her down for a few minutes, Mr. Arnold would use a long lead to tie Rose to a stake in the empty lot next to his house. He'd fetch a bucket of water and some oats in a pail. Back in his own yard, he would toss the pail into the feed bin inside the stable and drop the bucket by the well that he'd dug close to his house. Sometime in the evening Mr. Arnold would bring Rose back to her stall for the night.

Picking up the pails again, Mackenzie turned into his yard and hurried past the foul-smelling night-soil stewing in the concrete box closet. The box and its smell would not go away, he knew, until his family got water pipes and an indoor toilet. This waste would not be picked up until Monday, three days away. If the temperature stayed at nearly 100 degrees, as it had for the past week, the stench would only worsen.

The Daily Phoenix

FRIDAY, JULY 9, 1912

A. G. BARNES CIRCUS TO ARRIVE IN ONE WEEK

Strongman to Visit Saskatoon Tomorrow

One week from today the special train carrying the A.G. Barnes Circus will arrive in Saskatoon and the busy crews will begin setting up their tents and wagons for the performances set to commence on Saturday, July 17. No expense has been spared this year to bring the highest level of entertainment on the Barnes tour. Wild animals are featured on the program and more are presented at each performance than may be found in the combined menageries of any four other circuses.

Among the favourites will be Captain Richard Ricardo and his company of twenty-four monster African lions; Captain Stonewall and his bevy of seals; and Mme.Florine and her host of leopards, panthers, and jaguars. A half a hundred other performers will amaze and delight young and old alike.

Chief among these will be the Mighty Marmaduke, the Strongest Man on the Great Western Plains. By special arrangement with the A.G. Barnes Circus, the Giant Gypsy of Galicia will visit Saskatoon tomorrow to offer a free and fantastic demonstration of his powers. The Mighty Marmaduke will arrive on the Canadian Northern Railway and all curious citizens are invited to that station at one o'clock when he will tempt challengers to match his astonishing displays of strength.

CHAPTER TWO
Saturday, July 10, 1912

A small piece of red paper

THE NEXT AFTERNOON MACKENZIE UNFOLDED a sheet of wrinkled brown paper and flattened it on the dining room table. Beside it he set a ball of rolled-up pieces of string. He picked up a Hudson's Bay Company catalogue from the music rack of his mother's organ and sat down at the table. Opening the catalogue to a dog-eared page, he slid the tip of his finger over each of the twenty-six knives pictured. Any one of them, he thought, would be good for skinning off bark, whittling a branch, or carving a block of soft wood.

His mother came into the room and spilled an armload of his father's white shirts near the paper. Beside them she set down a square metal tin. Printed in chipped blue paint on the side of the tin were the words, "Snowflake Biscuits. Toronto Biscuit and Confectionery Company."

"What do you see for a new sweater for school?" she asked picking up a shirt and folding in the sleeves.

Mackenzie glanced up to see his mother smiling.

"A new outfit for your sister? Boots that might fit you through the winter? A lovely bonnet for your mother?" She lay the shirt on the paper and picked up the next one in the pile.

"I was only looking. I know I won't get one."

"Someday you shall."

Mackenzie flipped the page.

A few moments later his mother reached for the tin. Lifting the lid, she riffled through the envelopes inside. She took out one marked, "Laundry," and shook it to jingle a few coins. "I'd better make sure we have enough to pay for these, Mackenzie. While I do, fetch your father's collars for me, please. They'll be on top of his dresser. Mind you go up on tiptoes and don't wake your sister."

When he returned, his mother was holding up the last shirt. She took the collars and placed them on top of the pile, then turned and let the shirt drop onto a chair. It wasn't part of his father's laundry, Mackenzie saw, it was her good white blouse.

As she folded the brown paper over the shirts, his mother said, "I can give that one a good wash myself. It doesn't really need laundering." She unrolled a piece of string, wrapped it around the parcel and tied a bow. "And you know about the collars?" she asked. "Be sure to tell Mr. Lee your father doesn't like much starch."

"I think he knows." Mackenzie took the parcel. "Father said I could go see the Amazing Marmaduke from the circus."

"That's fine, but come home smartly. I plan to have tea with Mrs. Armsbitter this afternoon and I'll need you to watch young Nell."

Mackenzie grimaced.

NEAR THE DOWNTOWN END of the Traffic Bridge, Mackenzie discovered a crew of surveyors spiking lines of wooden stakes down the middle of the street. The route they were marking, he knew, would soon be laid in steel tracks to carry streetcars.

Lee's Laundry was a small white wooden building on Nineteenth Street in Saskatoon's Chinatown. When Mackenzie entered, a string tied to the door jingled a bell. Hot, wet air, smelly with the bad-egg odour of simmering coal, clung to his face like a sopping towel. Mackenzie joined a line behind two people at the counter. Facing them was a Chinese man Mackenzie hadn't seen before.

Just behind the counter were two tables. Each was about the size of the one in Mackenzie's house, except these were covered with bedding. Blankets had been laid over them, then a sheet drawn tightly over the blankets. The sheet was curled around the edges and nailed to the bottom of the table. Resting on top of each was a ceramic basin holding a shallow pool of water and a bamboo whisk.

Between the tables stood a stove. Three or four different-sized irons rested on either end of the scrubbed-steel stove-top. A few steps behind the tables a faded-green curtain hung across the back of the building.

The customer at the head of the line suddenly threw up his hands. "No tickee! No tickee!" he cried. "I know I have no tickee. It's in my room. Lost! Lost!" He turned an angry face on the woman waiting behind him and rolled his eyes. "No tickee, no laundry. What a way to run a business. If they just learned how to speak the King's English, they wouldn't get themselves in this mess!"

The woman backed up a step, bumping into Mackenzie. "Oh!" she gasped, then stepped to the side.

Leaning over the counter, the customer shouted, "Robinson! My name, Robinson. Does that help?" He straightened up. "No. Probably not."

The man behind the counter frowned. "What was washed?" he asked. "Tell me what was washed."

"Shirts!" the customer shouted. "Four or five shirts. Two pants. Maybe three. You said they'd be cleaned by now. What have you done with them?"

"Shame," the woman muttered. "That's not called for." She sidled further away.

The Chinese man walked to the nearest wall. Rows of paper-wrapped bundles, some stacked three high, sat on shelves. One after another, he picked up a bundle, studied its wrapping, and set it back down. Then he came to one that he squeezed and hefted in his hands.

He placed it on one of the ironing tables, untied the knot, and unfolded the paper.

"Let me see," the customer called. "No! That's not mine!"

Leaving the parcel spread open on the table, the man walked toward the curtain.

"Hey!" the customer shouted, pounding his fist on the counter. "Where are you going? You can't leave. You have to find my clothes."

The bell pinged as the door opened and the woman left the laundry.

The sound of one person and then another speaking Chinese came from the back of the store. Pushing through the curtain, the man headed back to the shelves. A second person glided through. It was a boy, a little shorter than Mackenzie and with straight black hair hiding his forehead. Stopping at one of the ironing tables, his eyes flicked between the Chinese man and the customer.

After sorting through a few packages, the man picked up one and returned to the counter. "Okay," he said, "this is it."

"What," the customer said. "How do you know? You didn't even look."

"This one," the man repeated, tapping his finger on some Chinese characters printed on the brown paper.

"Show me."

As the man started to untie the string, a voice floated out from behind the curtain. Immediately, the boy turned and stole out of sight.

"All right," the customer said, ruffling his fingers through his clothes. "Wrap them up again." He pulled a change purse from his pocket. "I don't know how you can keep going with your tickee this and tickee that."

The man took the customer's money, dropped the coins into the tin box kept under the counter, and returned some change.

Mackenzie stepped forward and undid the bow on his parcel as the door bell jingled. Mr. Lee, who owned the laundry, came through the curtain. He said something quietly to the man at the counter who turned and walked to the back of the store.

"For Mr. Davis, yes?" Mr. Lee said. Smiling, he picked up each collar and checked the inside for its small Chinese character. He did the same with the shirts.

"Good, good," he said, dropping everything on one of the ironing tables. "And not too stiff," he said, laughing and pinching his shirt.

From under the counter Mr. Lee took a small piece of red paper and on it neatly drew a Chinese character. "Keep this," he said and handed the paper to Mackenzie. Then he brought out a well-worn notebook and wrote quickly on one of its pages. "Mr. Davis can pay at the end of the month."

"Thank you." Mackenzie slid the paper into his pocket. "When will they be ready?"

"Monday. In hot weather they dry fast." Mr. Lee turned and called out to bring the boy into the store to gather up the shirts. When Mackenzie stepped outside, the woman who had fled earlier walked back into the building.

Mighty Marmaduke moves a boxcar

THE MIGHTY MARMADUKE stroked his neatly trimmed beard and twisted the pointed ends of his heavily waxed moustache. Like a billowing purple tent, his shirt hung loosely from his burly shoulders and barrel chest. A long black cord with tasselled ends cinched his black pants around his vast stomach.

Hundreds of men and boys and a few women had gathered near the Canadian Northern Railway depot. Some waited on the station platform. Others surrounded the strongman or stood nearby on the steel rails, wooden railway ties, and cinder-covered ground. The circle was broken by a hulking brown freight car. A few feet away towered a coal-black, ten-wheeled locomotive.

"Gentlemen!" a circus barker cried through his megaphone.

To gain extra height above the crowd, the barker had straddled the locomotive's cowcatcher. Behind him, a dozen boys perched even higher on the train engine's body or clung to her smokestack. From his roost above the wheels, Mackenzie spotted Albert nudging through the crowd. Albert spied his friend and clambered up beside him. He was wearing a clean shirt, Mackenzie saw. His hair was brushed. And the toes of his boots had been polished.

"Ladies and gentlemen!" Raising one arm of his bright red jacket like a priest about to bless his flock, the barker called again. He waited until those at the back stopped talking. "The event you have all been waiting for is about to begin. The challenge has been set." He whipped one arm toward the boxcar. A rope, thick as a man's arm, was knotted to the car's steel coupler. The rope dropped to the ground and lay like a sleeping African python for twenty feet along the railway ties.

"The Champion is ready. The Mighty Marmaduke now invites any man standing here today to try to match his strength and power. The Giant Gypsy of Galicia will with bare hands wrapped around this cord, cause this massive railway car to roll on its track. How is this possible, you ask? The Mighty Marmaduke you see before you today is the fourteenth in a line of Galician strongmen that can be traced back over three hundred years to the castled kingdoms of Europe. The guarded gypsy secrets that anoint the powers of extra-human strength have been passed from father to son for all those years and now rest in this Marmaduke, known as the Strongest Man on the Great Western Plains.

"Is there a man alive in Saskatoon who dares to think he can match this feat? Is there a challenger here who will step from your midst?"

A hum of voices rose from the throng then quietened when a man ambled onto the tracks. Shorter than the Mighty Marmaduke, the man was his equal in girth. Pulling a dark blue beret onto his head, he slowly made his way to the locomotive. There he held out his arm and shook the hand of the Giant Gypsy.

"Welcome to you, sir!" the barker called and all around the circle men cheered and applauded.

"Who's that?" Albert shouted over the din.

"Henry Lavallée," Mackenzie said. "People say there's no one stronger in our whole province. He owns the City Dray and does all the lifting by himself. My father watched him strap a six-foot bathtub on his back and carry it into the Great West Barbershop. One time Henry Lavallée wrapped his arms around a safe and hauled it up a flight of stairs to an office above Fairburn's Cigar and Billiards."

"Is that who you're betting on?"

"I would. Except I don't have any money."

"You'd lose it anyway," Albert said.

"Don't think so. There's a story that Henry Lavallée tied himself to a team of oxen once and wouldn't let them step an inch closer to their feed and water."

"That's not the same as moving a few tons of boxcar," Albert said. "My father saw Marmaduke do this in Minneapolis, Minnesota, and no one else could even budge the car." He turned to the boy on his other side. "Are you going to bet?" he asked.

The boy nodded. "Sure. I'll take Henry Lavallée."

"You're on," Albert said and reached into his pocket.

Raising his megaphone, the barker cried, "The rules, ladies and gentlemen, are simple and honest. In a show of incredible strength the Mighty Marmaduke will single-handedly move this railway car along the track. The challenger must then try to match that feat. If, gentlemen, *if* he proves successful, the challenger will then set the test for himself and the Mighty One. If both meet that test, it falls to the Giant Gypsy to raise the next bar. And so on until one man fails."

The barker held one hand at his chest, a finger pointing skyward. "Let me remind you, ladies and gentlemen, that this show is being offered to you absolutely free. You are seeing without charge one of the Circus Masters of the Great West, the Amazing Marmaduke. Our company, the incomparable A.G. Barnes Circus, will perform in your city one week from today. We will be most gratified to see each and every one of you and your wives and all of your children inside our Big Tent for our spectacular Three Ring extravaganza.

"But now –" he raised his hand over his head – "Let the show begin!"

The barker pointed to a man standing near the freight car. "The judge for today's contest," he said, "is the esteemed Mr. Mackasey, station master of the great Canadian Northern Railway. Mr. Mackasey will determine if and when his rail car has been moved by one

29

of these men. Now, please remain quiet. The Mighty Marmaduke must concentrate his whole body to the extraordinary task he has set."

The crowd obeyed. Pumping his arms and noisily sucking air into his lungs, the strongman paced across the circle once, twice, three times. Then he marched to the end of the rope. Facing away from the car, he wrapped the heavy cord two times around his shoulder and grasped the end in his huge hands. He crouched down, groaned like an old bull elephant, and strained. Settling back onto his heels, he took a couple of deep breaths, then leaned forward. Grunting loudly, he pushed himself far enough to fall forward one step.

"It moved!" Mr. Mackasey called. "I saw it clearly." A roar burst from the crowd as the Mighty Marmaduke flung the rope to the ground and strode away from the boxcar.

"It didn't move much," Mackenzie said.

"No one said it had to," Albert said. "It just has to roll a bit. Look at that giant, look at his arms. Your fat Henry is going to make a fool of himself."

The grinning barker calmed the crowd. Raising his hands, then lowering them as if he were pushing down a bulging blanket, he said, "And now the challenger."

Henry Lavallée walked to the rail car and studied the knot tied around the coupler. He stepped ten paces away, kicked at the cinders covering a few railway ties, and turned. He lifted the rope, hefting it in his hand. He draped the end over his shoulder and around his waist. Slowly he fastened a knot. Planting his feet against one of the ties, he stretched back until the cord tightened between him and the car.

For almost a minute, Henry Lavallée stood like that, as if he was leaning against an invisible wall. Then he grunted, bent his legs into a crouch, frowned, and pushed. Nothing happened. His face reddened and his frown deepened. He groaned. Still nothing happened. Bending lower, he slowly straightened his legs.

The cheer rose up before Mr. Mackasey, waving his arm, could declare that the car had moved. A man pushed through the throng hoisting a wooden keg over his shoulders. As the people applauded, the man set the keg down beside Henry Lavallée. The dray man unwrapped the rope from his body then slowly sank onto the keg as if it were a plush throne. He reached up to adjust his beret.

"He did it!" Mackenzie put the tips of two fingers in his mouth and whistled shrilly.

"That's just the first round," Albert said. "It's a tie. Marmaduke is still the champion."

The barker turned toward the Giant Gypsy of Galicia with a puzzled expression. When the Mighty Marmaduke shrugged, the barker raised the megaphone to his mouth. "Ladies and Gentlemen," he cried, "you have witnessed something rarely seen on the Great Western Plains. Not just one but a second Human Hercules has shifted tons of wood and steel entirely without assistance. And your entertainment is not complete. The challenger will now set his test."

Sitting on the keg with his feet apart and his hands on his knees, Henry Lavallée pursed his lips. He stood and walked into the swarm, sending men stumbling to the side in their rush to get out of his way. A wagon with glistening green paint and the words "City Dray" printed in creamy yellow waited at the edge of the throng. Two horses, one black, the other white, were hobbled and in their harnesses. Turning their big heads toward their master, they snorted. Henry Lavallée leaned over the side of the wagon and lifted something off the floor. He started back through the horde to where the Mighty Marmaduke waited.

Henry Lavallée was carrying two chunks of sod, the kind that homesteaders used to put up their first houses. Each piece was about a foot across, eighteen inches long, and three inches thick. Long prairie grass hung over the sides of the sod like golden hair. Henry Lavallée walked to the tracks and laid the pieces side by side on a tie. He leaned close to Mr. Mackasey and spoke to the station master for two or three minutes.

Mr. Mackasey nodded and held out his hand to the barker. When he didn't respond, the station master pointed to the megaphone. The barker slowly passed it over.

"Gentlemen," Mr. Mackasey said, "and ladies." He coughed to clear his throat. "Mr. Lavallée has asked me to explain the nature of his challenge. Before us on the ground are two squares of fresh prairie sod. In a moment I shall ask my friend –" he bowed toward the barker – "to confirm that they are identical. I will ask the Mighty Marmaduke to choose one of the pieces. Mr. Lavallée will take the other. Both men will be asked to hold the sod in their hands. At a signal from me, each man will attempt, with only his bare hands, to tear his square in two. The opening must begin on one side and go completely through to the opposite side. The first man to complete this feat will be declared the winner."

As the men around the circle shouted to one another, Mr. Mackasey lowered the megaphone. He looked at the barker and pointed to the sod. The circus man knelt down to lift and turn each piece then glanced up. The Giant Gypsy of Galicia snatched one of the chunks and grasping the edges, tried to jerk apart his hands. The sod didn't break. The Mighty Marmaduke frowned.

"What's going on?" Albert asked.

"My father told me about this," Mackenzie said. "Just watch."

Henry Lavallée picked up the other piece of sod. He held it in the palm of his hand, at waist height.

Raising the megaphone, Mr. Mackasey called, "Gentlemen! Gentlemen!" After some waiting, the audience grew quiet. "Your attention please. When I have counted down backwards, the two contestants may start. And may the strongest man win! Five-four-three-two-one – Begin!"

The Giant Gypsy pulled with all the strength in his shoulders and arms. With each failure to tear the sod, he looked more surprised and troubled.

Henry Lavallée lifted the square to chest height. His arm muscles bulged with the strain of tugging, while his fingers darted in and out of the sod.

"It's something about the roots of the grasses," Mackenzie said. "They've been growing for hundreds of years and are all twisted round and round each other. You can't pull them apart. You have to break them bit by bit."

A split opened in Henry Lavallée's square. As the Mighty Marmaduke strained desperately, Henry Lavallée's sod broke in two. When he raised the pieces over his head, one in each hand, a great cheer exploded from the circle. For the first time since the contest began, Henry Lavallée was grinning.

The Mighty Marmaduke threw his sod to the ground. Scowling, he began to leave, but the barker called to him and the Gypsy Giant returned. After shaking hands with the winner, Marmaduke slouched through the crowd behind the barker.

"He's never lost before," Albert said, slapping a coin into the palm of the boy beside him. "The next time some stubble-jumper tries to trick him, he'll be ready."

The two friends sprang from the locomotive and landed side by side in the cinders.

"What I really want to see is that lion tamer," Albert said, "Captain Ricardo."

"Would you ever do that? You'd have to be awfully brave. Have you seen how huge they are?"

"That doesn't matter. You just have to keep looking them in the eye. It's like taming mules. If you don't look away, they won't try anything."

"You won't catch me inside their cage."

"Where are you going now?"

"To the *Phoenix* office. I thought my father would be here, but I didn't see him. How about you?"

"Back to the ABC," Albert said. "Race you to Flanagan's. Johnny Hayes challenges."

"Tom Longboat, the great Canadian who runs faster than anyone," Mackenzie cried, "says it's a go!" The two boys shot out of the swarm mobbing Henry Lavallée and raced neck and neck down Twenty-First Street.

A black bowler and a grey cap

GASPING FOR BREATH, Albert and Mackenzie each hugged one of the columns that held up the roof over the sidewalk at the entrance to the Flanagan Hotel.

"Johnny Hayes," Albert said, "runs through the heat to win another marathon. London Olympics. July 24, 1908. Two hours. Fifty-five minutes. Eighteen seconds."

"You beat me," Mackenzie said. "But I was ahead until that rube rode his horse right in front of me."

"I was already catching up. You're just bellyaching."

"Next time," Mackenzie said, pushing away from

35

the column, "Tom Longboat will win." He took off his cap to wipe his forehead. "Come and look at this excavation with me."

The boys rounded the corner onto Third Avenue. After walking the length of the hotel and across the alley, they came to a row of wooden hoarding that ran along the edge of the sidewalk. At a break in the boards they stopped and peered down.

The pit was as wide as four houses, fifteen feet deep, and went from the sidewalk to the back lane. In a far corner, bathed in sunlight, three four-man crews slung pickaxes and shovels to break apart the dirt and throw it into deep-sided wagons. A teamster slouched on the seat of each wagon while his horses swung their heads low as if hoping to find a few blades of grass on the bare earth.

"My father says it's taking too long," Albert said. "Too many slow Stanleys like that bunch."

Mackenzie watched a man swing his pickaxe high over his head then drive its spike deep into the ground. He stood for a few seconds bent over the axe, both hands gripping the handle, the back of his shirt dark with sweat. Mackenzie imagined the man taking a deep breath. He saw him pull hard on the handle, then push it away from him. Back and forth and side to side the man thrust the handle until the spike loosened enough to be pulled from the ground.

"They're in clay," Mackenzie said. "They can't go any faster. It's not like digging in your garden."

"Well, my father's tired of waiting," Albert said. "He has people lined up wanting to move in. But he won't get a cent from the owner until they start paying rent."

One of the teamsters sat up, took the reins in his hands and called to his team. The horses strained into their harnesses. Slowly the wheels turned and the driver guided the team toward a wooden ramp built against one side of the hole. When the horses' front feet struck the bottom of the ramp, the teamster slapped the reins over their backs and shouted. The wagon crept up the slope.

"How many storeys is this one going to be?" Mackenzie asked.

"Six. There'll be a whole row of them along Third Avenue. When they're all built, you'll only see the sun at high noon." Albert raised one hand. "Johnny Hayes says, so long," he said. Albert turned back toward the Flanagan.

Mackenzie walked further down Third Avenue then into a lane that was a shortcut to the *Phoenix* building. The alley was rutted with wagon tracks and fouled with horse droppings. Boards broken from wooden crates and kegs had been thrown with spilled sawdust and packing papers against the backs of buildings.

Partway down the lane, Mackenzie spied three men standing close together. One of them stood on the step of an open doorway wagging a cigar in his hand as he talked. He had a round face and a bushy moustache that drooped over his mouth. A man in a faded-black bowler hat listened while shifting from foot to foot. The third man wore a grey tweed cap pulled down to his ears.

"Anything you get, you bring it to me," the man on the step said, sticking the cigar in his mouth and pushing his suspenders away from his chest. "You won't be sorry."

The one wearing the cap looked up and said something to the bowler hat. All three men turned and drilled their eyes into Mackenzie as he walked past.

"Right you are then, mate," he heard one of them say. "We'll be back. There'll be some business we can do together."

A moment later, one of the men spoke, his voice now right behind Mackenzie but well above his head. "A back alley's no place for a young younker," the man said. He jabbed his finger between Mackenzie's shoulder blades, hawked, and spit. As a gob of tobacco sailed over his shoulder, Mackenzie felt a smelly spray strike his cheek. "Get's awful dirty here. Wouldn't you agree, Lester?"

"Aye, certainly can get dirty," the other man said. Mackenzie heard a foot scuff the ground, then a chunk of dry manure drifted past his leg and broke apart a yard in front of him. "Dangerous, too." With that Mackenzie was jostled from both sides as hands slapped over his pants' pockets.

"Younkers would be best to stick to the streets, I'd wager," the first one said. "I expect this one knows that now. I expect we won't be seeing him back here again."

When he got to the end of the alley, Mackenzie

wheeled and, heart racing, headed toward Twentieth Street. He heard the men cackling loudly behind him. He remembered, without turning, exactly what they looked like.

Not another servant like that one

THE WOMAN SPEAKING TO MISS PRICE wore a pale yellow dress, a matching sun hat, and a woven straw bag. It was Mrs. Crawley, Mackenzie knew. Albert's mother had been away for awhile and he thought she probably wouldn't remember him.

"She has to be skilled, you understand," Mackenzie heard Mrs. Crawley say. "She has to care for my wardrobe, and help with the housekeeping, and look after the children when they're home. And she has to have some pride in what she is doing, for heaven's sake. Not like the last one. She didn't lift a finger and she felt no shame for it. We brought her all the way from England. My husband arranged it. For one full week she moped about the house saying this wasn't what she expected. Well, what else could you expect if you're in service? Then she informed me she was going to visit her sister who has some position in the retail trade. That's the last I saw of her. Two days later the sister sent the dray over to pick up her trunk. I swear they had it all arranged."

Resting both his hands on the counter, Mackenzie glanced around the office. The desks were empty. The door to Mr. Aikin's office was open and it, too, was empty. Mackenzie pulled a copy of *The Daily Phoenix* toward him. Dropping the tip of his finger onto the newspaper, he turned it slowly round and round. He wanted his father to be there so he could tell him about the men in the alley.

"That whole affair was a shock, you can imagine," Mrs. Crawley went on. "My family's never had less than a full complement of staff. My husband assured me we could manage with just the girl and the cook. But there wasn't even the girl. I knew then I had to return to Minneapolis for a time. Now my husband says we'll try again. But I couldn't possibly have another servant like that one."

"No," Miss Price said, touching the tip of her nose with her handkerchief. "I wouldn't think so. How about 'competent'? *Wanted. Competent maid to assist lady in all aspects. Apply Mrs. A.B. Crawley, 720 Broadway Avenue North.* Do you wish to mention a wage?"

"Well," Albert's mother said, "I believe that twenty-five dollars is more than sufficient, don't you agree? She will be living in our house."

Miss Price wrote while she was speaking, "*Wages: twenty-five dollars a month.* That seems perfectly clear."

"Yes," Mrs. Crawley said. "And thank you for your assistance. My husband asks that you send the bill to his office. He'll see that it's paid."

Mrs. Crawley walked to the door, and out.

Without looking up from her work, Miss Price said,

"Good morning, Master Davis." She tucked the handkerchief into her sleeve.

"Good morning, Miss Price." Mackenzie sauntered over to the front of the wicket. "Did my father go to see the Mighty Marmaduke?"

"Not exactly." Miss Price lay down her pencil, set one hand on top of the other on the counter, and looked at Mackenzie. "He said he was going to the station but he wasn't going to watch Mr. Marmaduke. He was going to watch the people watching Mr. Marmaduke."

"Why?"

Miss Price smiled. "I suppose we will have to wait for Monday's newspaper to find out."

Another Galician strongman

A SINGLE SHRILL BLAST from the steam engine's whistle called a break for the trencher's crew. Immediately the men moved together to talk, sat on a dirt pile, or leaned over the handles of their shovels. A few of the workers pulled out bags of tobacco and small, white papers and began to roll cigarettes. Once it was lit, a man took a couple of puffs from his cigarette and passed it to the worker beside him. After that one had sucked in a bit of smoke, he, too, handed it along.

In the midst of one group Mackenzie spotted his friend Stanley, his bone-handled knife hanging in a leather sheath from his belt. Two years earlier, Stanislav Murawsky had come to Canada with his parents and younger sisters. Standing almost as tall as the workers now, and dressed like them in faded clothes, he looked ready to accept the cigarette if it was offered.

Mackenzie snuck up behind the men. Just as he was about to knock Stanley in the back of his knees, his friend twisted round, grabbed him by the waist, and flipped him upside down.

"Hey, you big lunkhead!" Mackenzie cried, "Let me down."

"Down?" Stanley said, swinging him over the trench. "How far?"

"No!" Mackenzie took a swipe that missed Stanley. "You think you're Henry Lavallée? Put me down."

Stanley spun Mackenzie around and dropped his feet onto the ground. "I cannot be Henry Lavallée," he said in his slow, one-word-at-a-time way of speaking. "The Mighty Marmaduke, I might be some day. He's Galician, you know, like me. We are all Galicians." He nodded to the nearby workers. "And strong."

Mackenzie wriggled from his grasp as the steam whistle tooted twice.

"Back to work!" barked a man in a white shirt and tie. With his feet braced apart, he stood on a platform on the trencher. "You boys, get away from there!" he said. Then, "Good day, Mr. Torrie."

Mackenzie saw a man in a suit walk up to the other side of the ditch.

"We're making good progress," the man on the machine said. "But, I have to be on these gypsies every minute. As slow as slugs, they are. And lazy as skunks. And grousers besides."

"That's all the help you're going to get," the visitor said. "There's no one else who'll do this work."

"Yes, sir," the man on the trencher said. "We'll get it done, Galicians or no Galicians."

Stanley spit as he and Mackenzie walked past the men returning to their work. "They hate Galicians, those bosses," he said. "They tell lies about us. They say we are stupid. And lazy. But we are building their city." He shrugged. "Henry Lavallée did a trick. The Mighty Marmaduke should have won. No one is stronger than him."

"I didn't see you at the station," Mackenzie said.

"I was not there. I was hunting. Some men came here to tell us what happened."

"What did you get?"

"Two bucks. Do you want to see them?"

"Sure."

Stanley ambled down a back alley, then into a large grassy lot. Stopping by a clump of saplings, he knelt down and set aside some newly cut branches. Two brown rabbits sprawled on the ground, stretched out to their full length like sleeping dogs. One end of a short rope tied their hind legs together. A homemade bow and three store-bought arrows lay beside them.

"There's lots of meat on them," Mackenzie said. "Your mother will be happy."

Stanley grabbed the end of the rope and swung the rabbits over his shoulder. "I am going to sell more newspapers," he said. "The same ones in the morning. But now John will give me bundles of four different newspapers for the King Edward Hotel in the afternoon, even one from Chicago."

"How are you going to get all that over to the hotel?" Mackenzie asked, reaching down to pick up the bow and arrows. "I could help you carry them sometimes."

"I do not need help."

Mackenzie handed two arrows to Stanley, fitted the third to the bow, pulled back the string, and sighted across the lot. Stanley had told him once that when his family arrived his father got a job digging basements by hand with a pick and shovel. One day a dray hauling dirt and stones away from his work site rolled over and crushed him. Now his mother worked as a cleaner and sewed for other women in the small house she rented on the west side of the city. She wanted Stanley to stay in school but in the summer he was allowed to get a job. When he showed up at the *Phoenix* office wanting to hand out advertising dodgers, Mr. Aikin asked Mackenzie to show him which streets to go down. After they became friends, the two boys often saw each other when they met near a work crew.

Handing back the bow and arrow, Mackenzie said,

"All right. But if I'm around the station, maybe I'll come and see how you're doing."

We have nothing

AFTER SUPPER, Mackenzie's father wrestled a laundry tub up the basement steps to the kitchen. His mother poured two pails from their range's water reservoir into the tub.

Nellie bathed in the lukewarm water first, cooing with pleasure, then wriggling and squealing when her mother lifted her out. While she dried Nellie, Mackenzie wiped up the water his sister had splashed onto the oilcloth flooring. Then he took the baby to the parlour and let her push the squawking organ keys as he pumped the foot pedals. In the kitchen their mother added water and washed. As soon as she was finished, Mackenzie emptied the reservoir and climbed in the tub. He was grateful that his father bathed at the Great West Barbershop when he got his hair cut once a week.

Later, drifting to sleep in his upstairs bedroom, Mackenzie heard a pail scraping against the bottom of the tub. He knew his father was hauling the water outside to pour on the garden. His mother said something, then repeated it with a sharpness in her voice. Slipping out of bed, Mackenzie tiptoed across the hall. In Nellie's room, a steel grate covered a hole in the wood floor that opened into the kitchen below. Mackenzie stretched out face-down on the thick rug that lay beside his sister's bed. He linked his hands and rested his chin on his knuckles.

"You said it would be a year, Ted," his mother was saying. "One year from the time we arrived here. The city would lay their pipes and we would have water and sewer. Well, the city's done its job, hasn't it? There are pipes running right outside our door. But we have nothing. Nothing! Each week I wait for Mr. Casavant's wagon to deliver our water. I wait for the men to empty our wretched box closet. This is not how I want to bring up our children, Ted. We barely have enough fresh water for drinking and cooking. I have only a few tablespoons left over to wash our dishes, let alone do a proper laundry. It's awful!"

"More than a few tablespoons, surely."

"Not much! And you know perfectly well what I mean. It seems every day I'm sending Mackenzie off to Mrs. Bailey."

"It won't be too much longer. But it's not that we can't get water, Maude. The Baileys don't mind. And Mr. Arnold's well is always there. That's what he uses for laundry and washing."

"Mr. Arnold," Mackenzie's mother spoke each word slowly, "bless his heart, is a very generous neighbour. But he is courting death every time he draws water from that well. You've seen it. It's a few scant yards from his manure pile. In your own newspaper,

Ted, Dr. McKay warned about wells like that. That's how typhoid is spread."

"Not where we live, Maude. Dr. McKay was talking about other parts of the city. On the west side, mostly. You haven't seen the rooming houses over there crowded top to bottom with men. Or the tents on the edge of the city where families live for months, far from any kind of clean water or proper toilets. That's where people catch typhoid."

"I do not believe that disease cares a whit which side of the river it spreads to. And I will not put the lives of my children at risk by bringing water that could be unsafe into this house. Mrs. Armsbitter –"

"I know Maude, I know. It's tragic about the Armsbitter baby. We won't let anything like that happen. I just thought..." Mackenzie's father's voice petered out.

"Thought what, Theodore Davis?" his mother persisted. "That this would do for your family? That typhoid wouldn't enter your house although it struck all around you? You might as well hang an amulet over our door like they did to stop the plague."

"Soon, Maude. Soon we'll have enough money saved. We'll get the plumbing put in and the pipes connected."

"Yes," Mackenzie's mother said quietly. "Thank you." After a pause, she asked, "We really will, won't we?"

As his father mumbled something in reply, Mackenzie pushed himself to his feet and padded back to his bedroom.

TYPHOID EPIDEMIC ABOUT TO EXPLODE WITH HOT WEATHER

Cases of Deadly Typhus Traceable to Well Water Nearness of Pit Closets and Livestock Responsible

The season for the yearly typhoid scourge is upon us, and according to Dr. McKay, this year will probably see the same high number of cases if not more.

The medical health officer stated there are two chief reasons why typhoid breaks out in our city. These are well water which has become infected and box closets from which flies carry the disease. Water in shallow wells is easily infected by water travelling through sandy soil or above-ground from contaminated areas, according to Dr. McKay. The closer closets and livestock are to these wells, the more likely the water will be infected. Citizens should never be fooled by the appearance of the water. Time and again, the health department tests have found the very germs that spread typhoid in alarming numbers in water that looks clear and tastes palatable.

No citizen of this city needs to fall prey to this disease, the medical health officer stated, and it is clear what needs to be done. "I have asked the city that as soon as water and sewer lines become available in a district, a connection to those lines be made compulsory and box closets be made illegal. If these two simple steps are carried out, we will see a quick and permanent end to the typhoid disease in our community."

CHAPTER THREE
Monday, July 12, 1912

Gophers in their stew!

ONCE PAST THE PAINT CANS AT THE ENTRANCE to Douglas Hardware, Mackenzie was met by shiny steel padlocks and porcelain door handles, mousetraps, and two-foot-high bird cages made from heavy brass wire. He turned and found displays of carpenter's tools. At the end of a counter he came to a glass-doored cabinet and knelt down.

Seven boxes lay in a row across the top shelf of the display case. Each box was open and held a knife on a bed of dark blue cloth. In a whisper Mackenzie read the names on the box labels.

"Little Giant. Single-Blade Easy Opener. Two-Bladed Tip Top. Texas Toothpick. Three-Bladed Dakota Cowboy. Two-Bladed Gentleman's Companion. Pearl Handled Alberta Special."

The price tag on the cheapest single-blade knife read 23 cents. The triple-bladed Dakota Cowboy, with a handle made from buffalo bone, was $1.12.

Closing his eyes, Mackenzie imagined a blade clicking open and its sharp edge slicing like Stanley's hunting knife through bark and rope. He stood up. Mr. Douglas was talking with two men near the door. As he passed them, the owner glanced in his direction.

Outside, three men sat on a plank bench, their hands on their knees and their heads turned to look down Victoria Avenue. Like crows perched side by side eyeing a bauble dropped on the ground, the men studied the trenching machine, now only half a block from the hardware.

MACKENZIE WAS A FEW DOORS AWAY from the *Phoenix* office when Albert and his father left the building. Albert B. Crawley Senior was a squat man whose clothes fit loosely. When he walked he swung his arms and took big strides with his short legs. Balding on top of his head, he wore a fat gold band studded with diamonds on the ring finger of each hand. "Hello, there, Mack," he called.

Mr. Crawley stopped to look across Twentieth Street to the Empire Theatre. "That's the kind of show I like," he said, wagging his finger. "First there's some vaudeville, then one of those new moving pictures. Mrs. Crawley and I will go see that performance."

The Empire's castle-like entrance reached over the sidewalk. Tall pillars held a dome that protected the large curved doorway. Mackenzie read the sidewalk sign and frowned. "All seats reserved," it said, "75¢, 50¢, 25¢. First show 7:00 p.m."

"We'll find a pile of money today," Albert said. "Then we can go to the pictures whenever we want."

Mr. Crawley grinned. "Don't forget your old dad," he said. "I could find a nice little property for you to put that money into." Chuckling, he nodded at the boys and set off down the sidewalk.

"That's all he ever wants to do," Albert said. "Find a nice little property. Yesterday after church he took us out in his new Ford. I thought we'd go to the ballpark, or see if they're doing anything yet for the circus. All we did was drive out of town and follow a cow trail to see what's supposed to be some new lots. It's just a bunch of gopher holes. My mother and my little brother got so sick he had to keep stopping the motor car."

"We went for a walk," Mackenzie said, "to where they might build a new concrete bridge. If they do, it'll be gigantic."

Albert shrugged. "Yeah? Well I found another place to go under the boardwalk. This one you'll like."

"Where is it?"

"The other side of my father's office."

Two men were walking toward them along Twentieth Street. "I don't know if I should go," Mackenzie said. "I'm supposed to meet my father to do

51

some errands." When the men were a few steps away, Albert shouldered his friend into their path, darted to the side, and sprinted away. "To the ABC!" he called over his shoulder. "Eat my dust!"

ALBERT SLAPPED HIS PALM against the side of his father's office, then counted out loud until Mackenzie came running up. "Five seconds! Johnny Hayes beat you clean. Madison Square Gardens. 260 laps. November 26, 1910."

"Next time I'll whip you," Mackenzie said. Panting heavily, he leaned one hand against the office window. "Snap!" a new sign read. "Buy now! Sell later! Guaranteed to make money!" He followed his friend down the street, toward the river.

Albert stopped and pointed at a space about as wide as their shoulders between two stores.

"This is where we get in," he said. "It's plenty deep enough." He stepped between the buildings. "Take a look. It's a go, I tell you." Dropping to his hands and knees, he asked, "Which side do you want?"

"I don't care."

Albert flattened himself, pulled his body in, and wriggled to his right.

Mackenzie followed, then turned left. Like a turtle, he planted his hands beside his body and swung his head to one side and then the other. Finding nothing, he crept further. After three or four yards, he stopped. In front of him were signs the space under the boardwalk had already been explored. Perhaps a muskrat or ermine had wandered up from the river. Maybe a stray dog had found shelter there. Mackenzie knew that porcupines ventured into the city. And skunks. Whatever it was, it had left plenty of droppings. Mackenzie retreated.

The sound of voices reached under the boardwalk from somewhere on the street. Mackenzie recognized Eunice McMahon and Ruth Anne Hardcastle. The girls stopped a few feet away.

"They're like little children," Eunice said. "You'd think they'd grow up and stop playing in the dirt."

"I know," Ruth Anne said. "Their poor mothers must get tired of cleaning their clothes."

"Not one of their mothers," Eunice said stepping onto the boardwalk and scraping her shoes across the planks. "She's too fragile. She couldn't possibly wash clothes. She has her maid do that. If she can find one." Eunice giggled.

Mackenzie heard Albert grunt and waddle backward toward the opening.

"Well," Ruth Anne said, "the other one's mother doesn't even have water to wash. My mother says she has to beg for it from her neighbours. But still he gets filthy as a gopher every day."

"He should know about gophers," Eunice said. "His Galician friend kills them with his bow and arrow. And sometimes he gets to take one home."

"And his mother skins it." Ruth Anne moaned. "And she puts them it in their stew for supper!"

Both girls were laughing. "Oh," Eunice gasped, "please stop. You'll make me ill."

"Gophers in their stew!" Ruth Anne cried. "Gophers in their stew!"

Giggling, Eunice shrieked, "Stop!"

"You think you're so smart," Albert shouted. Rolling onto his back, he pounded his fists weakly against the bottom of the planks. "Wait until I get out there, Badger Breath. We'll see who's smart."

"Same for you, Four eyes," Mackenzie called. As near as he could tell, both girls were standing over Albert, stamping their shoes on the boards.

"I can see up there, you know," Albert called. "I can see everything. Stupid girls."

"That's rude!" Eunice cried. In a swish of skirts, she and Ruth Anne scurried onto the street.

"You're dirty!" Ruth Anne screeched. "Dirty!"

A handful of gravel clattered onto the wood, scattering dust and pebbles over the boys. By the time they wormed their way out, the girls were gone.

Quite a city

MACKENZIE WATCHED THE MAN reach up and clamp a finger and thumb onto each side of his hat brim. He tugged the edges up and down, up and down, until they seemed even. He lowered his fingers to his face and smoothed down the fine hairs of his moustache. One hand dropped to his tie. He nudged the knot slightly from side to side against the stiff white collar that rose to press against the bottom of his chin. He pulled the cuffs of his shirt past his jacket sleeves and brushed unseen bits from his dark pants. Raising his head, he discovered Miss Price, hands folded on the counter, studying him.

"Ak-hmm." The man cleared his throat. "I wish to place an advertisement," he said. "In *The Daily Phoenix* newspaper."

"Yes," Miss Price said, raising her hands to reveal a pad of yellow, lined paper.

"Wanted to rent," the man began. *"Furnished room for light housekeeping gentleman. Must be close to down-town."* He watched Miss Price writing. "I wouldn't normally object to living a distance away from my work," he said. "But I can't remain in the part of the city where I am now."

When Miss Price looked up, the man continued. "I had no idea people were expected to live like that. I'm from Ontario. I hold a position with the Bank of Hamilton. When I was transferred to the branch in Saskatoon, it was a total surprise that my circumstances would be so primitive. My employer provided me with a hotel room for one week. By then I was expected to have located my own accommodation."

He frowned and went on. "Nothing. There was nothing suitable. I was forced to move to a tent on the edge of the wild prairie which I share with five other men. The conditions are abysmal, you can imagine. The closest water is a quarter mile away. Ants and flies and mosquitoes are everywhere, inside and out."

Rubbing his hands together, the man said, "It's not like I'm some ditch digger who can live in the same clothes for weeks on end. I'm a representative of a financial institution." He leaned forward. "Did I mention 'modern' yet? It must say 'modern.'"

Miss Price touched her handkerchief to her nose. "I'll read what I have," she said.

"Hello, son."

Startled, Mackenzie jumped. His father laid a brown paper parcel on the counter and put on his jacket and boater.

"I slipped out earlier and bought the things your mother wanted," he said, pushing the parcel toward Mackenzie. "I'm off to see Mr. Mackasey." He lifted up the countertop and stepped through. "You may as well tag along. We'll see who's found their way to our railway station today." Reaching into his pocket, he handed some coins and a piece of red paper to Mackenzie. "That will pay for my shirts. I'd like you to pick them up on your way home."

Mackenzie and his father walked down Twentieth Street to First Avenue, where they were stopped by the tracks of the Canadian Northern Railway. The railroad divided the downtown into two parts, east and west. A short distance to his left, Mackenzie could see the steps to the footbridge that crossed over almost twenty sets of tracks to the west side. They turned right toward the station, where two days before Henry Lavallée had challenged the Mighty Marmaduke.

"They've finally stopped adding floors," Mackenzie's father said, pointing to the top of the eight-storey Canada Building. "When Mr. Bowerman began, it was to be just four. Now that the cornice is up, we have the tallest building west of Winnipeg." He shook his head. "It's quite a city we live in. Quite a city."

Horse-drawn buses lined the curbs by the main entrance to the station. Each brightly painted wagon displayed the name of a hotel. Through the open back door of one of them, Mackenzie saw red-cushioned benches that ran down the sides of the bus. Inside a family waited to be driven away. The young children sat on their knees peering out the windows. Glancing up, Mackenzie saw the family's trunks stored in the luggage rack on the roof.

On the sidewalk in front of the station doors, uniformed drivers called to travellers.

"Empress Hotel," cried one. "Quiet location. East side. New this year. One dollar, with breakfast."

"Hot and cold water. Private Bath," another called, waving his hand. "Only the finest furnishings. Two blocks away."

"Best offer for the economic traveller," declared another. "Temperance Hotel. Across from the Canadian Pacific station." A man waved and the driver reached out, grasped a handle, swung the man's metal case onto his shoulder, and strode toward his bus.

Just outside the doors, a boy was hawking newspapers. "Three for a nickel," he cried, waving the folded papers clenched in his fist. "Get them here. *Phoenix! Winnipeg Free Press!* the *Herald* from Calgary! Three for a nickel."

Following his father through the heavy doors, Mackenzie was quickly cooled, the way he was when he and Albert ducked into the back of an Arctic Ice wagon the driver had left open. A great crowd of people milled about in the lobby. Their voices bounded up from the smooth granite floors and bounced between the high walls like echoes in a canyon.

A porter appeared, splitting the throng in front of him. Pushing a stack of small trunks on his two-wheeled trolley, the Red Cap cried out, "Make way! Make way for the gentlemen! Make way, now!" In his wake came two men wearing dark suits and fancy homburgs. Mackenzie spotted a grey cap pulled low on a man's head as he elbowed his way closer to the travellers. He knew who it was.

Mackenzie turned to tell his father, but before he could speak he was jostled aside by a pack of roughly dressed newcomers. His mother's parcel fell to the floor. Mackenzie snatched it back. Each of them hauling a wooden case or a canvas pack on their shoulders, the men glanced about nervously.

"More Galicians," his father said. "They probably just landed in Halifax within the week. By tomorrow they should all have jobs. Cleaning a stable, most likely, or hauling bricks up a ladder."

Near the ticket counter, a man leaned against the wall, boxes and paper-wrapped parcels spread at his feet. Dressed in well-worn clothes, the man's face, neck, and arms were deeply tanned. Mackenzie's father tipped his boater to him. "He's a bachelor farmer," he said to Mackenzie as the man disappeared behind them. "He came to the *Phoenix* this spring wanting to place an ad for an ox. He was living in a sod hut then, but he may have a shack built by now. He probably caught the early train this morning so he'd have the day to buy supplies and enjoy a hot bath. Now he's heading back to his lonely house." He chuckled, wrinkling the skin around his eyes. "I expect the next ad he'll place will be in an English paper. For a bride." Mackenzie's father smiled and the two continued down a hallway that led to the doors to the platform.

A family with five children huddled together. Looking like he'd claimed that patch of floor for his homestead, the father glared from under the drooping brim of his hat at other travellers who happened too close. His wife stood beside him, a silver crucifix necklace hanging over her black dress. Her baby lay against her chest. The next youngest child sat at her feet gripping the bottom of her blue apron. The three older boys each wore an oversized dark jacket and a soft, floppy hat. Standing nearer their father, their tired eyes peered into the lobby.

"Those ones probably are just starting out," Mackenzie's father said. "They won't even have a soddie to go home to yet. They're probably wondering why they ever left their own country." He stopped in front of a closed door marked "Station Master" on the frosted glass window, pulled his watch from his pocket, read the time, then turned to Mackenzie.

"How did you get yourself so dirty?" he asked, swiping his palm across his son's chest.

"This is the time that Stanley picks up his papers," Mackenzie said. "I want to see if he needs some help."

"Fine. But go home right after." Mackenzie's father pointed to the parcel. "Your mother is waiting for those things." He opened the door and stepped inside.

Mackenzie caught a glimpse of a woman approaching the newly arrived family. In one hand she gripped a placard about the size of a newspaper page. The other hand she held out until the father shook it. The woman spoke to the family, then she waved for them to follow her. When they turned to leave, Mackenzie recognized Mrs. Crawley, Albert's mother. The placard in her hand read, "Women's Christian Immigration League."

Mackenzie pushed through the large doors that opened onto the platform outside the station. Walking to the freight area, he passed rows of steel-wheeled wagons, some empty, others piled with cream cans, boxes, and travellers' trunks. The freight room door was wide open, showing more goods stacked on the floor and along shelves inside.

Beside the door, surrounded by piles of newspapers, stood a tall, skinny boy wearing short pants and a short-sleeved shirt. Nearby, Stanley knelt on the platform counting the number of newspapers in a bundle. Straightening up, he nodded at the older boy who put a check mark in a notebook he held. Then, like an officer in the army, the boy stood with his feet apart and his hands clasped behind his back. Rocking onto his toes, the boy was able to stretch a few inches taller than Stanley. When Mackenzie joined his friend, the boy turned away.

"Who is that?" Mackenzie asked. "Is he your boss?"

"His name is John Diefenbaker. He is not the big boss. But he hires boys like me to work for him. He is going to attend the university this year. He says he talked to the prime minister once. And that some day he will be prime minister."

"Next!"

"That is what he says. I believe him. He is smart enough."

Shaking his head, Mackenzie said, "I wouldn't bet on it." He reached down to slip his fingers through the string tying one packet.

"I can do it by myself," Stanley said. "I did this morning."

"But you only have half as many in the morning," Mackenzie said. "If you try to carry all these and spill some, they'll get wrecked."

"I do not need help." Stanley reached for Macken-zie's bundle.

Mackenzie stepped back. "I don't want any of your money," he said, "if that's what you're thinking."

"You want to buy a pocket knife," Stanley said. "You need money for that."

"I'll find some way." Mackenzie bent down, and keeping a finger looped in his mother's parcel, snatched a second bundle from the platform. "I'm ready," he said.

THE STEEL STEPS took Mackenzie and Stanley up to the footbridge that stretched for two city blocks over the Canadian Northern's tracks. The rail lines that passed underneath were later spliced together like strands in a braided rope until, a quarter-mile away, a single set crossed the river on the C.N.R. train bridge.

Walking slowly ahead, Stanley checked over his shoulder. Mackenzie hustled to catch up. Halfway across, they stopped. Mackenzie dropped his bundles and laid his parcel on one of them. Beside him, Stanley held onto his newspapers, lifting one bundle chest-high, then lowering it and raising his other hand. Up and down his hands moved, like the pistons on a slow-moving locomotive.

Turning north, Mackenzie admired the massive brick warehouses that rose on either side of the Canadian Northern tracks like the yellow and brown walls of a deep valley. Beyond these buildings, scattered houses were springing up on new roads that cut through the farmers' fields on Caswell Hill.

"This city's spreading out all over," Mackenzie said. "I don't think it can get much bigger. My father says that twelve years ago, when I was born, not even 200 people lived here. Now there might be 30,000."

"Where were you born?"

"In Winnipeg."

"Our train stopped at Winnipeg when we came here. The big Union Station reminded me of the Wawel Cathedral in Krakow, with just as many people inside."

"Is that where you were born?"

"No. In a village near Krakow. My mother wanted to go to the Cathedral when we knew we were leaving. It is the resting place of our patron saint." Stanley smiled. "Saint Stanislav."

"That's who you were named after?"

Nodding, Stanley lowered both hands to his hips. He lifted one arm until it pointed straight out from his shoulder. He let it drop to his side and raised his other arm. Mackenzie grabbed his bundle and the boys set off.

The west side of Twentieth Street began at the King Edward Hotel, one hundred feet from the bottom steps of the footbridge. The boys put down their newspapers at the entrance to the hotel.

Stanley slipped his hunting knife from its sheath and cleanly sliced each bundle's cord. He pocketed the lengths of string, replaced his knife, and started to work. "Get your paper!" he cried. "Right here! *Daily Star! Daily Phoenix!* Motor boat rides on the river! Another C.P.R. train wreck! Read about it here."

"I'll be back tomorrow," Mackenzie said.

Stanley stepped toward a man who had stopped to take out his change purse.

"Have you got a Chicago paper?" the man asked. "Give me one."

The strongest man

MACKENZIE HIKED along the centre of Nineteenth Street, a brown paper parcel gripped in each hand. Between the two lines of stakes left by the surveyors, he felt safe from the buggies and wagons that rolled noisily past and the sputtering cars that wove between them. He followed the wooden pegs as they curved away from Lee's Laundry onto Third Avenue and toward the Traffic Bridge.

A team of two horses, their harnesses jingling, came up behind him. A man's voice called out. "Is your mother still playing her organ?"

Mackenzie turned to find a black and a white horse plodding beside him. Each horse's harness sported a set of steel horns, glistening silver shafts that rose from the horse's shoulders and held shiny balls at their tips. Henry Lavallée looked down from the seat of his shining green dray. The top of the front wheel, with its

thick wooden spokes and a steel rim around the outside, was up to Mackenzie's shoulder. The back wheel
stood almost over his head.

"Yes," Mackenzie said. He remembered the day his
family had arrived in Saskatoon. Henry Lavallée had
carted all their furnishings from the station to their
house. The last thing carried in from the dray was his
mother's organ. As soon as it was settled in their parlour, she had played Henry Lavallée "Buffalo Gals,"
"The Old Grey Mare," and a couple of other songs.
"But she hasn't used it much since my sister was
born."

"Of course," Henry Lavallée said. "The baby will
keep her busy. Are you going home now? Yes? Jump up.
You can ride with me."

Clicking his tongue to stop the team, Henry
Lavallée shifted his vast bulk to the side. Mackenzie
passed up his parcels then scrambled to the seat. The
space beside Henry Lavallée didn't look much wider
than the big man's hand. Feeling like a squirrel
sharing a log with a bear, Mackenzie squeezed in.
Henry Lavallée handed the parcels back, then
clicked his tongue, and the horses dipped their heads
and set off.

"Can you take the reins?"

"Sure," Mackenzie said, turning to lay the parcels
on a wooden box behind him. He reached for the long
leather straps. As their hands touched, Mackenzie's fist
looked small enough to be swallowed up inside Henry

Lavallée's, like a baseball inside a mitt. Feeling the weight of the reins that led to the huge horses at his command, Mackenzie smiled.

The black horse twisted his head back and cast a wary eye toward the wagon seat.

"He's frowning at me," Mackenzie said.

"That's Blackie. He'll be all right," Henry Lavallée said, linking his hands across his big belly and leaning back. "He just likes to know what's going on."

"What's the white one's name?"

"Star. He doesn't care who has the reins. He just likes to keep moving."

Peeking up at the dray man, Mackenzie said, "I saw you beat the Mighty Marmaduke."

Henry Lavallée's eyelids dipped slightly and he nodded his head.

"I have a friend who is Galician, like Marmaduke," Mackenzie said. "When he grows up, he says he wants to be stronger than you."

Henry Lavallée chuckled. "We'll see." Then frowning, he asked, "What is this friend's name? Maybe I should be worried about him."

"Stanley. Or Stanislav."

"Stanislav." Henry Lavallée whistled and the wagon halted below a sign at the entrance to the Traffic Bridge. "Walk your horses," it read.

"Stay here," Henry Lavallée said, tugging his beret. With a grunt, he swung himself over the side of the wagon and walked to the front of the team. He grasped

Star's halter and started across the bridge, pausing each time they met an automobile.

On the far side of the river, Henry Lavallée climbed back on and talked his horses up the Short Hill. "Well done, gentlemen," he called as the dray cleared the top and rolled onto Victoria Avenue. The teamster steered his wagon along the side of the long ditch and past the trencher and the chuffing steam engine. As they rolled by Douglas Hardware, he shouted a greeting to the men sitting on the plank bench.

Henry Lavallée guided his team off the street and onto a cluttered space in front of a row of partly built two-storey houses. "Whoa!" he called, then draped the reins over the front of the wagon.

"They're going up faster than weeds in a slough," Henry Lavallée said. "Last year this was still wild prairie." Mackenzie turned toward the houses.

Each was covered in rough shiplap boards. At the nearest one a crew of men was unrolling strips of black tarpaper and nailing them to the walls with rapid taps of their hammers. A neatly-stacked pile of yellow bricks as high and wide as the wagon waited nearby. On the front porch a carpenter turned from his work, straightened up, and waved his long wooden plane at Henry Lavallée. The man brushed tightly curled wood shavings from his tie and white shirt, then reached into the pocket of his leather apron for a pipe.

"Cecil! Norman!" The carpenter called to two men slowly ripping a saw through a wide plank set on two sawhorses. The men stopped and pushed their shoulders back to stretch. "Give Henry Lavallée a hand with the nail kegs, boys." The carpenter struck a match over the bowl of his pipe. "He's had enough – hard work – lately," he said between puffs, then blew out a stream of smoke.

The drayman climbed down from the wagon and walked to the back. When the carpenter's helpers joined him, he hoisted a keg and set it on one man's shoulder, then did the same for the second. He pulled two more kegs to the back of the wagon and carried them like short, fat pigs, one under each arm, into the house.

Mackenzie picked up his parcels and leapt to the ground. "Thanks for the ride," he said when the big man returned to the dray.

"My pleasure. Say hello to your mother and father." From his apron Henry Lavallée took a well-worn pad with a sheet of purple carbon paper curling out from between two pages. He licked the tip of a sharpened pencil and began to write his bill.

"I will." Mackenzie said. He walked to the front of the team, reached up, and patted each horse on its granite forehead.

The Daily Phoenix

MONDAY, JULY 12, 1912

PICKPOCKETS AT WORK AROUND C.N.R. DEPOT

Light-Fingered Gentry Warming up for Circus Crowds

That a gang of pickpockets is operating in the city is absolutely certain and further that their favourite hunting grounds are the railway depots. In the past two days alone, three complaints have been made to C.N.R. officials: the first by a man who claimed to have been relieved of $100, the second by a traveller who said that he was robbed of $60 and a leather pocket book, and a third by a man who lost two rings which he carried in a jeweller's gift bag. A significant fact is that not one of the three can give any information that might lead to an arrest.

A representative of *The Daily Phoenix* newspaper attended the demonstrations of strength performed by the Mighty Marmaduke of the Barnes Circus and local drayman Henry Lavallée on Saturday with the intention of catching any light-fingered gentry at work. While the police received reports of many lost items following that exhibition, no pickpockets were seen in action. All of this points to the culprits being highly skilled in the nefarious art.

Chief Dunning is of the opinion that this gang is warming up for the thousands of unsuspecting homesteaders, rubes, and travellers who are expected to arrive in our city this weekend to attend the annual visit of the A.G. Barnes Circus and he cautions everyone to keep a hand on the moneybag at all times.

CHAPTER FOUR
Tuesday, July 13, 1912

The typhoid, again

THE CAB DRIVER REINED IN THE TEAM PULLING the dark blue Beaton's Taxi coach. Turning in the seat high above the front wheels, he said something through an open window to the passengers. Then the man jumped to the ground, put a hobble on one of his horses, and walked toward the *Phoenix* building. Swishing their long tails over their haunches, the matched white horses held their heads high like a king and queen viewing their realm.

Mackenzie followed the man into the office. Just inside the door, the cab driver took off his cap, brushed his hand over his blue uniform, and bellowed, "Ted!"

Miss Price's head jerked up from the paper on which she was writing. Mr. Aikin leaned to the side of his desk to see who had caused the ruckus. With his back to the door, Mackenzie's father raised his hand briefly but continued typing until he had reached the end of his sentence. He spun round in his chair.

"This is for you, Ted," the man said, shaking two pieces of paper clenched in his fist. His voice carried across the room. "It's from Doc McKay. I was picking up a fare at the hospital and he asked if I'd get it to you. He says its confidential, for only you to read."

When Mackenzie's father stood up, Miss Price dabbed her nose and spoke quietly to the woman outside her wicket. Mr. Aikin reached for the cigar tipped into his ashtray. He took a puff, squinted through the grey smoke at the cab driver, then replaced the cigar and picked up his pencil. Mackenzie's father took the papers from the cabbie and flattened them on the countertop.

"It's sad news," the driver said, "terrible sad. The doc said they lost another wee one. This one not yet two years old. The typhoid, again."

"Hmmm," Mackenzie's father said, lifting the paper to read the bottom sheet.

"And that's the particulars about the wee lad," the driver said. "For the death notice."

Mackenzie frowned, remembering the Armsbitters when Philip died.

"Its a Galician family, sure as not," the driver went on. "You can tell by the name. I swear some of them aren't fit to be parents. It's no wonder they get the typhoid. I wouldn't give my horses the water their kids have to drink."

"Shame," muttered the woman talking to Miss Price.

"Aye," the cab driver said, turning toward her. "A crime is what it is."

"Thank you, Raymond," Mackenzie's father said. "I can reach Dr. McKay on the telephone."

"He's got to do something, that Dr. McKay," the woman in line spat out. "Or somebody has to. Her children should be taken away. Or the whole family sent back to where they came from. No Canadian mother would give her children dirty water."

"It's not that easy, of course," Mackenzie's father said, "to know if the water you're using is safe or not. Even Dr. McKay's assistant has to look through his microscope to tell if there are any bad germs in it."

"You know the city water is safe," the woman said, setting her bag on the counter in front of Miss Price. "Anyone who cares would have that water piped in." With a sniff the woman threw her head back and pulled her change purse from her bag.

"Aye," the driver muttered, whipping his cap onto his head. "My fare's waiting in the cab. They need to catch the Grand Trunk." He nodded to Mackenzie's father. "Good day," he said and pushed open the door.

Why is that man talking so much?

AMBLING ALONG THE BOARDWALK, a man spotted the sign in the window of ABC Land Sales. He veered toward the entrance, sending Albert and Mackenzie scrambling to the sides of the steps. When the door opened, Mackenzie saw Mr. Crawley spring from behind his desk, his arm held out in front of him.

"Come on in," he cried. "I'll show you those lots. I've got the map right here." He patted a tall table with a top that sloped upwards like the roof of a house. Reaching past his visitor, Mr. Crawley flicked the door closed. Albert and Mackenzie settled themselves on the steps.

"What's the Immigration League?" Mackenzie asked.

"The what?"

"I saw your mother yesterday at the Canadian Northern station. She had a sign that said 'Women's Christian Immigration League.'"

"Oh, that. My mother joined some other ladies who want to help people who come here and don't know what to do. Some of them can't even speak English. They take them to the Immigration Hall, find them a place to stay, things like that. And then they bring them to our church."

Albert stood up. "This place I want you to see is over on First Avenue across from the tracks. Soon they're going to take out that boardwalk and build concrete sidewalks. Now's the time to get in there and find the money."

"That's what you say," Mackenzie said. "But I haven't found one thing so far." Looking up at Albert and the bright, cloudless sky surrounding his face, Mackenzie held an arm across his forehead. "What about Badger Breath and Four Eyes?" he asked. "How do they keep figuring out where we are?"

"I don't know." Albert said. "But they won't find us this time."

A gang of seven or eight young boys swirled around the corner near McMahon's Dry Goods. Yelling and laughing, they formed a circle with someone stuck in the centre. When they got closer, Mackenzie saw that the person in the middle was the Chinese boy from the laundry. Wearing a blue smock and baggy black pants, the boy carried a pole slung over one shoulder. A green cloth bag as big as a tied-up bedsheet hung from each end of the pole.

Soon Mackenzie could hear the words the boys were shouting.

"Washee, washee, Chinaman,
Use your soap and suds.
Here's your tickee, Chinaman,
Give me back my duds!"

Over and over they repeated the verse, waving their hands as if they held something between their fingers. At the end of each refrain they burst into laughter and slapped their knees.

The Chinese boy stepped off the sidewalk and crossed the street. With the gang still noisily surrounding him, he mounted the boardwalk near where Mackenzie and Albert sat watching. The boy slipped the pole off his shoulder, turned sharply, and entered Harry Tupling's Men's Furnishings. The boys in the gang stood outside, sniggering and wrestling, until two of them followed the Chinese boy into the store.

"What's going on in there?" Mackenzie wondered.

"Delivering laundry," Albert said. "What do you expect?"

"But how? He can't speak English." Mackenzie stood up. "Have you ever been in Harry Tupling's?"

"Once, about two days ago. My mother bought me an ugly knee-pant suit that I'm telling you I will never wear." He picked up a rock, tossed it in his hand, and stared across the street as if he was searching for someone to fire it at.

Mackenzie noticed then that Albert was wearing another set of clean clothes, his blue shirt still creased where it had been folded in the shop.

"Has your mother hired a maid yet?"

Albert narrowed his eyes and stared at Mackenzie.

"I was in the *Phoenix* office when she placed an advertisement. I'm just wondering."

"Yes. Finally. Now she can stop buying me new clothes. My old ones are good, but she wouldn't let me keep wearing them until she hired someone to wash them."

The door to the men's store swung open and the two boys from the gang stumbled into their friends' arms.

"I'll come back with my father," one of them shouted through the closing door. "Whenever I please."

Mackenzie started toward the store. The boys in the gang clumped together and shuffled noisily toward Third Avenue.

The first steps into Harry Tupling's were like a walk into a vast clothes closet. Mackenzie was surrounded by racks of overalls, boxes of work gloves, shoes and boots, shelves of white shirts, collars, socks, and ties, and hundreds of hats and caps hanging from hooks against the wall and stacked ten or more high on tables.

The Chinese boy was standing at a counter at the back of the store. A man on the other side of the counter, wearing a high collar and a black jacket, stopped talking and eyed Mackenzie. Tall and thin, the man stood with arms akimbo. He had a long beak of a nose and a sharp Adam's apple.

Ichabod Crane, Mackenzie thought, remembering the schoolteacher in the story, "The Legend of Sleepy Hollow." He picked up a box of high collars. The man lifted a shirt from a pile on the counter and continued talking.

"Tell your uncle he has done a superb job, as usual," the man said. He dropped the shirt and picked up another, fingering the ends of the sleeves. "No one in this city can repair clothes the way he can. No one."

Mackenzie peeked toward Ichabod. "If you come back on Thursday," the man said, "I'll have more work for you. I know Mr. Tupling will be very pleased."

76

The boy waited silently with one hand gripping the pole that stood beside him like a knight's lance. Why, Mackenzie wondered, is that man talking so much? He's wasting his breath on a Chinese boy who doesn't understand a thing he's saying.

"And this is my own laundry?" the man asked, undoing the second green bag. "Wonderful. Wait a moment and I'll get your money."

When Mackenzie saw that the man was coming his way, he reached for a tie.

"Yes?" the man asked.

Mackenzie looked up to see Ichabod, his thin lips pressed tightly together, gazing at him through hooded eyes.

"Those are not what a boy would normally wear," the man said, then curled up the ends of his lips.

"I know," Mackenzie said, "but ..."

"But you were a little curious, perhaps?" Ichabod said, tilting his head. Leaning forward, he frowned at Mackenzie. "You aren't one of those brutes taunting the laundry boy, are you?"

"No!"

"Good," Ichabod said, straightening up. "But scoot anyway. There's nothing more for a curious boy to see." He took a few steps away, then turned back to Mackenzie. "Go!" he said, raising his eyebrows.

Mackenzie did as he was told and joined Albert outside.

That will bring you good luck

WHEN HE REACHED FIRST AVENUE three strides ahead of Albert, Mackenzie rapped his fingers against a steel lamppost and spun round.

"Tom Longboat," he said, "by seven seconds. Boston Marathon. April 19, 1907. Two hours. Twenty-four minutes. Twenty-four seconds." He caught his breath and held out his open hand. "The winner will collect his prize."

Albert took a penny from his pocket and set it on his thumbnail. "Heads you get the king's money," he said and flipped the coin. "Tails you get a medal." He snatched the falling coin and slapped it onto his wrist. "Tails." Albert stepped toward the rail line that ran along the side of the street.

Fifty yards down the tracks, a switchman unhitched the last boxcar in a line strung behind a locomotive. With a blast of its whistle, the train engine shuddered, then rumbled toward them. Kneeling, Albert set the coin on top of a steel rail.

When the last car had passed, Mackenzie picked up the flattened coin and rubbed it between his fingers.

"That will bring you good luck, Mack," Albert said, laughing. "Don't lose it."

On the far side of the street stood a livery stable, a two-storey building with weathered wood siding and an open barn door. A groom led a mare outside and tied her beside two other horses close to a trough of water. After patting the horse's flank, the groom crossed to a smaller building next door and disappeared into the dark, smoky inside.

The boys walked over and peered through the doorway of Blondin's Blacksmith shop. The air swirling out was hot, brown, and smelled of smouldering coal. Flames burst from the darkness as someone cranked a bellows. The light flickered orange against the leather aprons of two men leaning over the forge. Grasping a pair of tongs, one smithie lifted a red-hot length of iron and swung it over an anvil. With his other hand, he rang the head of a large steel hammer down on the iron.

Backing out of the doorway, Albert and Mackenzie skirted around the horses to the boardwalk on the far side of the stable. When the way was clear, they lay down in a little gully and wriggled under the planks.

Mackenzie crawled for ten feet before he stopped and flopped on the ground. He opened his fist to study the penny in a bar of light streaming through a crack. The king's face was squished, but on the flip side he could make out the word "Canada".

Two voices overhead began talking about riding. They've come from the livery stable, Mackenzie decided.

"Thunder is such a gentle horse," one girl said. "He never complains. He never gets excited."

"I know," a second girl said. "And he's clever too. He can tell me what he likes and what he doesn't like."

Mackenzie heard a horse neigh as if he were joining the conversation.

"What he's telling me right now," the second girl said, "is that he wants to turn around. He's tired of facing this way. He wants to see everyone going down the street."

Mackenzie knew who was talking. It was Badger Breath. The other one would be Four Eyes. He clenched the coin. This time he could hear what they were saying, and they wouldn't know he was listening. He smiled, thinking what he would tell Albert in a few minutes.

"Hold him, please," Eunice said. "I need to fetch something."

"Good boy," Ruth Anne squeaked, sounding nervous to have the horse at arm's length.

"Okay, Thunder," Eunice said. "You can turn around. That's a good boy," she cooed, "right against the boardwalk."

A shadow had fallen across the crack. Mackenzie twisted his head up. He could see the hind quarters of a horse looming above him.

"Oh dash it," Eunice said, "I just remembered. Whenever I feed and water Thunder after a ride, he always ..." She didn't finish. Then, "He always ..."

"That's all right," Ruth Anne said, "he's just following nature."

"I know," Eunice said, "but I just hope he doesn't do it on the boardwalk."

Mackenzie dug in his elbows and frantically scurried backwards. He didn't get far before a loud splat struck the boards above him and a pool of warm liquid washed over his neck and back.

"Oh, dear," cried Eunice.

"Get that horse away from here!" Mackenzie shouted. "You can't let it do that."

"Is that poor boy under the boardwalk again?" Eunice said. "If he didn't spend his time gawking up at people from down there, he wouldn't get so dirty, would he?"

Ruth Anne giggled. "I'm sure I don't know what he's complaining about," she said. "It was just a bit of water from the horse trough."

"You're not funny," Mackenzie grumbled.

TWENTY MINUTES LATER, Mackenzie tramped out of the *Phoenix* office with his father close behind.

"I didn't think you could get any filthier," his father said, "but it seems you can. Your mother will be fit to be tied when she sees you."

Before he could swat Mackenzie's clothes they heard a sharp clatter of breaking glass. Two men dashed across the Second Avenue intersection.

"It's at Syman's," one of the men called to a third standing on the sidewalk. "A car's backed through the window!"

Mackenzie glanced at his father. "Another one! Let's –"

"You're not going anywhere. Except home to get yourself clean."

"But –"

"No buts. Get!" Mackenzie's father turned to the *Phoenix* office. "I'm fetching my notebook," he said. "And when I come back out, I expect to see you on your way."

"Will you write a story?"

"Possibly. Today's newspaper is already put to bed. If I write something for tomorrow you'll see it then. Now, off with you!"

Dragging the toes of his boots across the cracks in the boardwalk – thunk, thunk, thunk – Mackenzie headed to the bridge.

Every boy needs a knife

ONCE MORE IN CLEAN CLOTHES, Mackenzie opened the door to the hardware. Mr. Douglas walked through the opening from a storage room and followed Mackenzie to the knife display.

"Is there something you've got your eye on, son?"

"A knife."

"Sure. Any one in particular?" Mr. Douglas pulled a key ring from his trousers pocket. He fit a small key into the cabinet's lock. "Here's one about your size," he said, holding out a Little Giant. Mackenzie pulled out the larger blade, clicked it open, snapped it back into the handle, and tried the smaller blade.

"Did you want to buy that one?"

"I don't have any money," Mackenzie said, handing it back.

Mr. Douglas replaced the knife and snapped the cabinet lock shut. "Well, I can't really help you then, can I? Talk to your father. Tell him every boy needs a knife. Away you go, then."

I am not afraid of failure

MACKENZIE WATCHED from the station platform as Stanley took a fifth bundle from John, knelt, and carefully counted the newspapers. When Stanley looked up and nodded, John made a tick in his book.

Stepping closer, Mackenzie asked, "Is it true that you spoke to Sir Wilfred Laurier?"

"Yes," John said.

"When?"

"Two years ago, less two weeks. July 29, 1910." John looked down the platform. "Not one hundred feet from where we're standing."

"What did you talk about?"

"We spoke at length about matters of the day. Then we each wished the other well and went about our business. Sir Wilfred was to give a speech later that day at the university. I had my newspapers."

"And you told him that you are going to be Prime Minister too?"

John fixed Mackenzie in his gaze. "I did. And I will."

"How can you be so sure?"

John clasped his hands behind his back and rocked up on his toes. "It has to do with failure," he said. When Mackenzie frowned, John continued. "And success." He pointed one arm and wagged a finger at Mackenzie. "I am going to be Prime Minister," he said, "because I am not afraid of failure. Everyone knows that I spoke with Sir Wilfred. What they don't know is how often I tried before I was successful."

He swung his arm behind his back again. "The city was expecting Sir Wilfred. There was to be an official welcome and many events. Bunting hung from the lampposts. No less than if the Governor General himself were making an appearance. I decided that I would speak with him. The morning after his train arrived, I waited on the platform outside his special coach. Sir Wilfred was busy. He didn't leave the train. That afternoon I waited too, but there were important people for him to meet and places for him to visit. In the evening I also waited, but there was a banquet and Sir Wilfred returned very late.

"Most people would have given up after all that, but I did not. Early the next morning I arrived at the station. With my bundle of newspapers at my feet I stood beside the tracks. Sir Wilfred came out onto the small platform at the back of his coach for some morning air. When he saw me, he beckoned me over. And we had our chat.

"You see, it doesn't matter how many times you fail. It matters only if in the end you succeed." John smiled. "Which is why someday I will be Prime Minister. I am not afraid of failure." He spun round and with his hands still together behind his back, paced toward the freight room.

"You don't say!" Mackenzie muttered. Nudging one of the bundles with his toe, he asked Stanley, "Why are you taking extra newspapers?"

"I need to make more money," Stanley said. He stood up, carrying three bundles balanced against his chest. As he shifted the weight in his arms, Mackenzie noticed a piece of soiled white cloth wrapped around his friend's finger and fastened with an elastic band. A dark red circle stained the cloth.

"What happened to your finger?"

"I cut it. I poked it with my knife when I was skinning a rabbit. It does not hurt." Stanley flexed his fingers. "I am going to find a better job. I told my mother I am going to stop going to school."

"She won't let you," Mackenzie said. "She wants you to get an education."

"Not any more," Stanley said. "Everything costs too much. We do not have enough to buy food for my sisters or pay our rent."

"Where will you get a job?"

"Somewhere," Stanley said. "Give me one more."

"Another bundle?" Mackenzie asked. "Why?"

"I want to see if I can carry four."

Mackenzie snatched the two remaining bundles and carefully lowered one onto Stanley's pile. "Can you do it?"

"Yes." Stanley set off down the platform.

Mackenzie swung the last stack onto the top of his head. Balancing it there with his fingertips, he caught up with his friend, who was slowly lifting his linked hands up to his chest, lowering them, and lifting, over and over.

"Do you want to go to the circus on Saturday?" Mackenzie asked. "My father might have some free tickets."

"I would like to see the Mighty Marmaduke," Stanley said. "He –"

A long, piercing blast of a train whistle cut off Stanley and drew a rush of people through the station doors. As a conductor called, "All aboard!" Mackenzie slowed down for passengers to pass in front of him. Glancing toward the train, he recognized a man standing on the steps to a Pullman coach. It was one of the men he'd seen in the back alley, the one with the grey cap.

A passenger approached the steps but was blocked when grey cap turned his back to him. The traveller tried the other end of the coach, but was stopped again, this time by the man wearing the faded black bowler. By now grey cap had climbed down and come up behind the traveller. He bumped his shoulder into the passenger's back, then quickly turned and headed into the station. Black bowler jumped down to the platform, leaving the passenger to enter the Pullman.

Pickpockets! Mackenzie thought, as he watched the two men disappear through the station doors. They're the gang that's been robbing people around here. I'll tell Father, he decided. He can write a story for the *Phoenix*.

"All aboard!" the conductor cried. He lifted a set of wooden steps from the platform, tossed them lightly through the door to the coach, and hoisted himself up.

The train jerked, the steel wheels squealed into motion, and the cars began to roll slowly down the track.

A bank of dark clouds tumbled over the station. Shivering, Mackenzie pulled the newspaper bundle from on top of his head and hurried to catch up to Stanley.

The bucket lay on its side

MACKENZIE DROPPED HIS PACKET near the steps to the King Edward Hotel and watched the first drops of rain smudge the top newspaper.

"You are going to be soaked before you get home," Stanley said.

"What about you?"

"I will be all right. When it rains they let me stand in the entrance. But," Stanley looked up as a crack of thunder ripped across the sky, "I will not sell many newspapers."

"Tom Longboat outruns the wind," Mackenzie cried, spinning round and sprinting toward the railway overpass.

He was still dry when he took the Short Hill steps two at a time. Breathing heavily, he gripped the stairway railing at the top of the hill and looked back across the river. A mile-wide waterfall of silver rain plunged from the black clouds swirling over the downtown. One-two-three flashes of forked lightning stabbed into Caswell Hill. Mackenzie loped down Victoria Avenue until, as he passed Douglas Hardware, the wall of rain overtook him and instantly he was drenched. Slowing to a walk, he splashed through puddles and skidded over slick mud.

"Race cancelled," he said, blowing drops of rain from his nose. "Due to the weather."

Arriving home sopping and cold, he changed into what he had worn earlier in the day, and draped his wet clothes over a line behind the range. His mother had already started the fire. Mackenzie checked to see that the woodbox was full, then picked up Nellie and sat in the rocking chair. His sister held his hands and practiced jumping on his legs.

"It could be night for how dark it is," his mother said, fastening some loose hair behind her ear with an amber shell barrette. "Set a lamp for me, Mackenzie. And we'll need more water too."

Mackenzie sighed. "Right now?"

"Yes. The rain will finally put some water in our cistern. But that will take awhile. I need the water for supper."

With both hands straining over her head, Nellie reached for her brother's cap. "It's awfully wet," Mackenzie said, leaning forward.

"Mack!" Nellie cried, seizing the hat and pulling it into her face.

Mackenzie hoisted his sister into her high chair and slipped his father's oilcloth rain jacket from a peg. He picked up two pails and shoved his feet into his rubber boots.

"Remember to say thank you to Mrs. Bailey," his mother said.

"Yes." Mackenzie pulled the door closed behind him.

A strong gust pelted fistfuls of rain down his neck. He snugged the jacket around his chin and followed the mucky trail across the garden and past the box closet. He peered along the back alley toward Bailey's. Rippled brown puddles spread over the lane, filling the deep ruts of wagon wheels. Mackenzie sloshed straight across the alley and through the open door of Mr. Arnold's barn.

Rose swung her head out of her shadowed stall as Mackenzie squeezed by the wheels of Mr. Arnold's buggy. Setting the pails on the wooden planks of the barn floor, Mackenzie roughly rubbed the horse's head and pulled his fingers through her mane.

"Hi, Rose," he said. "You glad to be inside?"

Through the door leading to Mr. Arnold's house he could see the round cover of his neighbour's well. The bucket lay on its side on the wooden lid, its rope coiled loosely on the ground nearby.

"It would be such a snap," Mackenzie said as if he were talking to the horse. "I could fill those pails in no time." The picture of the little coffin flashed before his eyes and Mackenzie sighed. "But, I won't."

He chucked Rose under her chin and bent down to pick up the pails. Working his way past the buggy he lowered his head into the wind and started down the back lane.

The Daily Phoenix

TUESDAY JULY 13, 1912

$100,000 Worth of Smoke and Water-Damaged Merchandise

MUST BE CLEARED OUT

There is no profit in this for us, only glory and hard work. Our sole object is Quick Clearance to make room for the carloads of brand new goods already here and on the way hurried through by eastern manufacturers the minute they heard of our misfortune.

Our entire regular staff, with an army of extra help, are still hard at it, trying to evolve order out of chaos. It's a Herculean task, but they are doing nobly and on

Wednesday, July 14th,

the Doors of this Store will be thrown open to the
Biggest Money-Saving Event in the History of Saskatoon.

Space permits only this short list of some of the high-class Merchandise to be sold.

Thousands of dollars' worth of Laces and Embroideries.
Thousands of dollars' worth of Gloves and Hosiery.
Thousands of dollars' worth of Neckwear and Ribbons.
Thousands of dollars' worth of Mens' and Boys' Clothing.
Thousands of dollars' worth of Dinner Sets, Tea Sets, Fancy China Pieces, and Glassware.

In conclusion, we ask the ladies to accept this friendly piece of advice: "Do not wear White Skirts." The present State of the store is our misfortune, not our fault.

J. F. Cairns, Second Avenue, Saskatoon

CHAPTER FIVE
Wednesday, July 14, 1912

Thundering neck and neck

"RIGHT THIS MINUTE," MACKENZIE'S MOTHER said as she watched him lift Nellie's perambulator over the last step from the basement, "people will be streaming down Second Avenue. It's like the Fair. Your father says that there'll be hundreds coming off the trains from villages and farms all around."

Mackenzie took a bag that held two of his sister's milk bottles and a tin box with their sandwiches and stowed them on the rack under the pram. With its rounded front and long, low bed, the wicker body looked like a toboggan on wheels.

It seemed to Mackenzie to take almost an hour to walk down the Short Hill, across the Traffic Bridge, and along Second Avenue. Hopeful shoppers filled the sidewalks and the street in front of the Cairns Store, blocking all traffic.

"People were lining up well before nine o'clock," a woman exclaimed to Mackenzie's mother.

He went up on tiptoes. Each large window of the store showed off a different display: ladies' clothes, men's clothes, furniture, and shoes of all kinds and sizes.

"You'll have to take Nell," his mother said. "They'll be no room for the pram inside the store. Come back for me in two hours. Give her a bottle if she gets hungry."

Scowling after his mother had left, Mackenzie muttered, "I'm not a girl." He pushed the pram toward the curb, then bounced it roughly onto the sidewalk. Frowning at Nellie, he parked the carriage outside the Jones Emporium and walked a few feet away. He crossed his arms, leaned against the wall, and didn't look at his sister.

Nellie began to fuss. Mackenzie spun the carriage around and hurried down the sidewalk. He shoved the handle of the pram hard enough to make it roll ahead of him. When he caught up to it, he peeked at Nellie, who lay on her back whimpering, then launched it again. At the end of the block, he grabbed the handle just before the wheels dropped over the curb onto Twenty-First Street.

The sound of shouting rose from somewhere further along Second Avenue. Suddenly the people walking on the street stopped, cried out, and fled toward the sidewalks. A runaway team galloped toward Mackenzie.

Alone in the wagon, a boy tugged frantically on the reins.

Mackenzie shot a glance toward the Cairns Store. Shoppers still filled the street, keeping watch on the queue creeping into the building. His mother stood on the near edge of the throng. Cupping his hands around his mouth, he shouted, "Runaway!" He felt his voice get sucked into the noisy hubbub.

As the wild-eyed team tore toward the intersection, a green wagon rumbled onto Second Avenue from Twenty-First Street. "Heyah! Heyah!" the driver called. "Go, boys! Go!"

His feet braced wide apart, Henry Lavallée slapped the reins over his horses' backs. Moments after Blackie and Star reached the avenue, the runaways raced alongside.

Alerted finally to the sight of the two teams thundering neck and neck toward them, the Cairns shoppers stampeded toward the sidewalks, desperately butting like frightened cattle into those in front of them.

With a crack of splintering wood, a front wheel on the runaway wagon shattered. Instantly, that corner tilted wildly groundward. With nothing but the reins to clutch onto, the boy slid from his seat toward the whirling wheels of Henry Lavallée's dray. The teamster reached over the side of his wagon, wrapped his arm around the boy, and hauled him across his knee.

Henry Lavallée pulled fiercely on his reins as the dray swerved to block the frightened team. The runaways halted within yards of the milling shoppers.

In the few seconds of calm that followed, Mackenzie was jolted by his sister's piercing screams. Red-faced and with her tiny fists clenched, Nellie rocked angrily on her back. Mackenzie lifted her to his chest and reached under the pram for her bag. He held the milk bottle to her lips. His sister sucked on the nipple, but after a few gulps, she pushed it away and cried out. When she refused the bottle again, Mackenzie cupped his sister's head under his chin and bounced her gently in his arms. His mother burst from the mob flocking toward the two teams. With a worried look at Mackenzie, she held out her arms for Nellie.

"I've never been so frightened!" his mother cried, running her hand through the loosened hair at the side of her face. "I didn't know where you were."

"I could see you," Mackenzie said. "You were right where the horses were heading."

"For a while I was. Then I was able to get to the sidewalk. It was terrible being in their path and not able to move."

"Henry Lavallée saved that boy," Mackenzie said. "And then he stopped the horses."

"He's a hero, no doubt." Mackenzie's mother held her whimpering daughter away from her chest. "What's wrong with Nell? Has she been crying? Did you feed her?"

"I tried. She only took a couple of sips." Mackenzie picked up Nellie's bottle and handed it to his mother.

When the baby refused the milk, she asked, "How long has she been flushed like this?" She held the back of her hand to Nellie's forehead. "She's hot as the dickens. Did you have her in the sun?"

"No. We were on the shady side of the street. She's been like that the whole time."

Sighing, his mother kissed Nellie's cheek. "I'll get you home," she said. To Mackenzie she added, "Stay with me as far as the bridge. My heart won't calm down." She laid Nellie in the pram and gently pushed the carriage. "I'm sorry your sister was fussy. But really, it wouldn't be so awful looking after her for an hour or so, would it? I think that on Saturday she'd love to go with you to the circus."

MACKENZIE FOUND HIS FATHER sitting on the curb talking with the boy from the runaway wagon. A woman stood on the other side of them, staring down at the ground and dabbing her eyes with a handkerchief. The broken wagon and Henry Lavallée's dray were nowhere to be seen.

Mackenzie's father patted the boy on the shoulder, stood up, and shook the woman's hand. Turning, he spotted Mackenzie. "Everyone all right?" he asked, slipping his notebook into his pocket and his pencil behind his ear.

"Yes," Mackenzie said. "Did you see the runaway?"

"I was on my way to the Hub when Henry Lavallée whipped his team onto the avenue." Mackenzie's father laughed. "I had to run to keep up."

He nodded his head over his shoulder at the boy. "He and his mother had come into town to pick up some supplies. The father was busy on the farm. The boy's been driving the team since he was old enough to walk, so they figured he could handle the city. It was a motor car, again. It got too close to the horses, back-fired its engine, and away they went. The boy feels terrible, of course. They lost a wagon wheel and maybe an axle. They won't be going home tonight. Still, they were darn lucky that Henry Lavallée was around."

"Where's their wagon?"

"Some men loaded it onto the back of the dray. They took it to Blondin's Blacksmith shop."

"The men did? What about Henry Lavallée?"

"He was hurt. Something's wrong with his shoulder. Dr. Croll came over from his office and he convinced Henry Lavallée to go to St. Paul's Hospital. I don't expect that they'll keep him there very long, though."

"Why were you going to the Hub?"

"Work." The skin around Mackenzie's father's eyes crinkled. "Maybe you could help me." He steered them down the sidewalk. "I'm gathering some information for a story about our city's ice cream appetite. The people at the Hub Confectionery tell me they've got a new machine they'd like me to look at."

"What do you want me to do?" Mackenzie asked.

"We're going to inspect that machine," his father answered. "And then we're going to do some testing to see if it's all it's cracked up to be. Will you give me a hand?"

"That's a cinch!" Mackenzie suddenly remembered he hadn't told his father about the pickpockets. "And I've got news for you," he said. "I think it'll make a good story."

Get off my sidewalk!

MACKENZIE LEFT THE HUB with the fresh taste of strawberry still in his mouth. When his father stopped to talk to people waiting in the line outside, he waved goodbye. Soon he was snaking across streets and down back alleys on his way to the Canadian Northern station. A few feet down a lane off Twenty-First Street he stopped short. He'd taken a wrong turn.

On the step of an open doorway a man stood in his shirt sleeves, his thumbs hooked around his suspenders. He had a round face and a bushy moustache that partly hid the short cigar stuck between his lips. Pulling a watch from his pants pocket, he checked the time, frowned, and peered both ways down the lane.

He's waiting for the pickpockets! Mackenzie thought. He spun round and bolted back to the street. Wheeling onto the sidewalk, he saw grey cap and black bowler sauntering toward him. Immediately he ducked into the entranceway to an office building and pressed his face into the stone wall. Behind him a door swung open. The Chinese boy from the laundry stepped through and turned into the path of the two men.

"Onto the street with you, you little navvy."

Peeking around the corner of the entranceway, Mackenzie watched black bowler swipe at one of the boy's green bags and knock him sideways.

"Out of our way!" grey cap called, grabbing the pole and flinging it and the bags to the ground.

Chortling, black bowler punched grey cap on the shoulder. "It's time you learned some English," he barked to the boy. "'Out of the way' means get off my sidewalk." He flung both arms toward the startled boy who stumbled backward off the curb. Grey cap kicked the bags after him. Laughing, the two men continued down the street.

As he ducked back into the entranceway, Mackenzie caught a glimpse of a tall, thin man running toward the Chinese boy. Ichabod Crane was waving his arms awkwardly, like a teacher trying to break up a schoolyard fight.

"We don't need that sort messing up our city, do we mate?" Mackenzie heard black bowler say as the men passed behind him. "Send them all back to China, is what I say."

When Mackenzie left the entranceway, Ichabod and the Chinese boy were gone.

She's deathly sick

MACKENZIE TURNED from Victoria Avenue onto Ninth Street East in time to see a shiny dark blue car pull away from in front of his house. Recognizing Dr. Weaver's automobile, he raced home.

His mother paced the kitchen floor, her dark brown hair falling over her damp forehead and flushed cheeks. She held Nellie in her arms, the baby's head lolling against her shoulder.

"Why was the doctor here?" Mackenzie asked.

"It's Nell, can't you see? She's deathly sick. She can't keep a thing down. I thought it was the heat but it's something worse. The doctor will be back tomorrow morning. If she's not better..." She raised Nellie to softly touch her lips to the top of the baby's head.

"She'll get better." Mackenzie drew his hand down Nellie's back. When he wriggled a finger into her armpit she whimpered but didn't move.

"Maybe she needs a toy to play with," he said. "I could make her something."

"She's too sick to play. You could chip some ice from the block. That will at least cool her. And you shouldn't be so close, Mackenzie. You could catch the infection too."

"How did she get it?"

"I wish I knew. Dr. Weaver thinks it might have been bad water. But I don't know how that could possibly be. I swear every drop we use comes from either Mr. Casavant or Mrs. Bailey. It's all city water. I don't know what's making her sick or what might make her better."

THOROUGHFARE WAS STREWN WITH PRECIOUS STONES

Jeweller's Loss Will Top $2,000

Thousands of dollars worth of diamonds and other precious stones were scattered over the street when a delinquent automobile ploughed through the window of A. Syman, jeweller, about two o'clock yesterday afternoon. Witnesses to the altercation told *The Daily Phoenix* reporter that the machine responsible had been left backed against the curbing on Second Avenue near Twentieth Street, in the reverse gear. When the operator, Mr. Jack Petit, came out to crank it, the car immediately started on the backward move and quickly reversed up on the sidewalk and through Mr. Syman's window.

In an effort to assist Mr. Syman, Mr. Petit promptly engaged the automobile's motor and drove it back across the sidewalk. This display of neighbourliness kept most of the gathering crowd of onlookers at a distance but also succeeded in scattering the contents of the window in every direction.

A large crowd soon collected, which was kept in check by Sergeant Devereux and Constable Skinner. The debris was carefully brushed into a pile and the mixture carried into the store where the particles were examined under a microscope to make certain none of the smaller diamonds were thrown away. Mr. Syman could only conclude that a quantity of the larger jewels had been stolen. In all, Mr. Syman's loss to theft in the incident likely will reach the vicinity of $2,000.

CHAPTER SIX
Thursday, July 15, 1912

Something for Nellie

THE STICK LOOKED TO BE AS THICK AS HENRY Lavallée's finger and twice as long. Mackenzie had discovered the young tree uprooted in the back alley. After dragging it into his yard, he had used the family axe to lop off a piece of straight branch. With one of his mother's knives, he'd peeled back the green bark to expose a pale slimy skin that had soon dried and hardened.

In his mind, Mackenzie saw smoothly rounded ends, deep grooves that circled the limb and a carved N near the middle. Although he pressed with all his might, the knife left barely a dent in the wood.

His mother walked onto the stoop behind him. In her hand she held a full baby's milk bottle. Nellie was slumped in the crook of her arm.

"Where on earth did that tree come from?" she asked, tucking loose hair behind her ear. "Did you drag it over my garden? Take it back where you found it, Mackenzie." She started down the steps, stopped and cried, "Mackenzie Davis! What do you think you're doing with that knife?"

"I'm making something for Nellie," he said. "A toy."

"Not with one of my bread knives, you're not." She held out her open hand. "Mackenzie?"

He laid the knife in his mother's palm.

"What am I supposed to use?"

"I can't think about that right now. Your sister is sapping every bit of energy I have. You'll just have to use your imagination, I suppose." Mackenzie's mother turned and went back into the house.

Slipping the stick into his pants pocket, Mackenzie clomped off the steps. As he leaned down to grab the sapling, his mother came back onto the stoop. "She's like a little dishrag, all hot and wet from the wash water. Come in and chip more ice for me." Heading back inside, she added, "And then get changed so that you can go downtown. I have some errands for you."

Reaching under his collar, Mackenzie pulled out the flattened penny that hung around his neck on a length of string. He caressed the coin, rubbing his thumb over the sharp edges around the hole he'd pierced with a nail. Then he dropped the penny under his shirt and stood up.

THE PIPE WAS DISAPPEARING into the trench, one heavy piece at a time. Teams of two men lifted each section, waddled with it slung low to the ground between their knees, and lowered it into the hole. As the piece dropped, four arms reached up and guided it down. A man wearing a jacket and homburg hat strode along the edge of the trench, barking orders to the workers below.

Mackenzie walked past the foreman, then veered toward the trench. As he was checking the hole, Stanley came up behind him.

"I was wondering if you'd be around here," Mackenzie said. "Did you go hunting already?"

Stanley nodded. "As soon as my morning papers were sold. I got a nice, big buck."

"Good shooting. My sister's sick, Stanley. I can't help you this afternoon. I have to stay around the house."

"I will be all right. I can lift all five bundles now, anyway. What is the matter with your sister?"

Looking down at his feet, Mackenzie said, "We don't know for sure. She has a terrible fever. I think she's getting worse."

"That is bad," Stanley said. "My mother is always worried about my little sisters. But she has some medicine if they ever get sick like that. She makes it from a recipe my grandmother gave her before we left. It tastes terrible, but it takes the poisons out of your body. Do you want me to get some for you?"

"No thanks," Mackenzie said. "I'm going to Campbell's Pharmacy right now to buy something."

Sooner or later they all get a haircut and a bath

ALBERT POINTED to an unpainted wooden building with a row of little windows that ran along each of its two storeys. "A rooming house," he said. "It's called the Willet."

Nearby stood a smaller structure with the red, white, and blue stripes of a barber pole painted on a sign. The letters B,A,T,H,S were written one under the other down the side of the pole.

A barefoot man wearing a white undershirt and pants held up by suspenders came out of the barbershop. Carrying another pair of pants and a shirt draped over one arm, he walked along the boardwalk and into the rooming house.

"I was here yesterday with my father," Albert said. "He had to get some papers signed. While I was waiting, I saw a man, just like that one. About halfway back to the Willet, some coins fell out of his pants pocket. He got down on his hands and knees to pick them up. But I know some of them fell through because he put his eye down to the crack. Then he swore and slapped his hand on the plank."

Albert smiled. "My father says there are about a hundred Galicians crammed into the Willet. Sooner or later they all go over and get a haircut and a bath." He rubbed his hands together. "This will be our gold mine, Mack."

"I can't stay," Mackenzie said, turning away. He held up a small, dark-green glass bottle. "I have to get this home. Nellie's really sick."

"Let me see that," Albert said. He read the words on the label. "'Prince Rupert Drops. A reliable family remedy for pains of all kinds.' Holy smoke! Look at this. It cures coughs, colds, croup, bronchitis, asthma, dysentery, diarrhoea, summer complaint, catarrh – what's catarrh? – cholera, headache, piles, spasms, frost bites, burns, and scalds." He tossed the bottle back to Mackenzie.

"There's typhoid fever in the city right now, you know," Albert continued. "My mother's always harping about it. If she ever thought we might really catch it, she'd have us out of here faster than you can say Minneapolis, Minnesota." He kicked a stone off the boardwalk. "Race you?"

Mackenzie shook his head.

"I say we'll find at least one buck each under that boardwalk. Bet me?"

"No."

"Did you hear about Henry Lavallée? He's strong enough to move a boxcar but he hurt himself lifting up a boy."

"That's not funny. He really is hurt. My father says he might not be able to work for awhile. Anyway, Albert, I don't feel like laughing right now."

"All right, all right." Albert was quiet. Then, "Hey, here's something you'll like. Remember on Tuesday, when the car crashed into Syman's? I was coming back from taking a letter to the Empire Hotel for my father. I heard the Ford go through the window. Right away a bunch of people ran toward the jewellery. And who do I see coming out? Stanley! Darned if your friend didn't bolt out of the door and hightail it down the sidewalk faster than a scared rabbit."

Mackenzie stopped. "Stanley? He was inside Syman's?"

"Yep. Slow Stanley. I'd never seen him move that fast."

"What would he be doing in there?" Mackenzie wondered out loud.

He is a person no different than you or me

MACKENZIE SPOTTED THE GREEN BAG hanging from the end of a pole as it poked through the doors of the Drinkle Building. The Chinese boy swung past the sidewalk sign for the Great West Barbershop and headed toward Chinatown. Mackenzie followed.

Near Twentieth Street a gang of boys swarmed out of an alley. They circled the Chinese boy, punched his bags and shouted:

"Washee, washee, Chinaman,
Use your soap and suds.
Here's your tickee, Chinaman,
Give me back my duds!"

Mackenzie stepped warily across the street. One of the attackers grabbed a bag and hung on it until the pole sprang from the boy's shoulder and the bags fell to the ground. Like a pack of coyotes, the boys charged, kicking the bags until laundry spilled through the openings.

"Stop that!" a woman demanded, stepping onto the sidewalk from the Saskatchewan News Agency. Raising her clenched fists to her hips, the woman stared at the gang members as Mackenzie stopped a few paces behind the Chinese boy. He recognized Mrs. Crawley.

"You ought to be ashamed of yourselves," she said. "You've no right to torment another human being so. No right at all. I'm sure this boy has done nothing to wrong you."

Mackenzie cast his eyes down to the blue towels lying at his feet.

"He's just a Chinaman," one boy griped. "There's no harm."

"He is a person," the woman said as Mackenzie looked up, "no different than you or me. And you will treat him as such."

Her eyes fell on each boy in turn. She raised her arm, pointing toward the mouth of the back lane. "Now, get!"

Sharing surly looks, the gang members slouched around the side of a building and out of sight. The Chinese boy squatted down and gathered in the loose laundry.

Mrs. Crawley studied Mackenzie, her eyes narrowing. "You're the Davis boy," she said.

Mackenzie nodded as the woman walked closer to him.

"Albert told me about those young hooligans," she said. "I believe they should be reported to the police." Mrs. Crawley looked both ways down the street, as if expecting to see a constable nearby.

"Help me with these," she said, kneeling. Mackenzie reached down and picked up a couple of towels which he handed to Albert's mother when she stood up. Mrs. Crawley passed them to the Chinese boy. He tied up the bundles, hoisted the pole to his shoulder, and set off again toward the laundry.

"Now, that wasn't so difficult, was it?" Mrs. Crawley said, smiling at Mackenzie and tugging down the cuffs of her sleeves.

Seven open boxes

MEN'S LAUGHTER drifted into the hardware store from the sidewalk. Mackenzie glanced toward the door then back to the display case. Seven open boxes were lined up on the top of the cabinet, as if Mr. Douglas had taken them out to show a customer, then forgotten to return them.

Mackenzie picked up the Gentleman's Companion, squeezed it, and let the knife's cool weight sink into his palm. Fitting his fingernail into the thin slit on the longer blade, he unfolded the steel until it snapped open. He pushed it shut, pulled out the shorter blade, then glided it back, too. He returned the knife to its box and stepped back from the display case.

A picture came into Mackenzie's mind of his sister whimpering in her bed, her face flushed and her skin steaming. The image changed. Nellie was sitting up, smiling, and cooing at a carved wooden toy she held in her hand.

Mr. Douglas entered the store and led one of his helpers into the back room. Mackenzie scooped up the knife box, put the lid over the top, and slid it into his pants pocket. He quickly walked outside.

$75 REWARD OFFERED IN DIAMOND HEIST

Police Ask Assistance to Nab Light-Fingered Thieves

A reward in the amount of $75.00 has been offered by Mr. A. Syman, jeweller, for information leading to the return of a quantity of rings and loose diamonds stolen from his store in a daylight raid two days ago. The theft apparently followed immediately on the destruction of his plate glass window by an automobile which raced across the sidewalk in a highly delinquent manner. It took some minutes for Mr. Syman, assisted by two police officers who arrived soon after the event, to gather up the scattered mixture of debris and jewels and it was in that time that the robbery is believed to have occurred.

Sergeant Devereux believes that this is the work of a gang of light-fingered scoundrels who are prepared to commit such a crime in broad daylight and in the midst of a considerable crowd of onlookers.

The police are of the opinion that the criminals may have suffered some injury, however slight, during this offence, due to the fact that the items they stole would have been scattered amongst plentiful shards of broken glass. Persons with information that could lead to the recovery of the stolen goods are asked to visit the police station and speak to Sgt. Devereux.

CHAPTER SEVEN
Friday, July 16, 1912

Running like Tom Longboat

T HE DAY HAD STARTED WINDY AND WARM AND had quickly grown hotter. A sheen of sweat glistened on Mackenzie's forehead as he sprinted between the lines of stakes leading to the Traffic Bridge. His boots pounding out bursts of dust, he was Tom Longboat running the Toronto Island fifteen-miler. June 21, 1912. In his fist he clutched a rolled-up copy of that morning's edition of *The Daily Phoenix*.

HEAVY INFANT MORTALITY DRAWS ATTENTION TO IMPURE MILK SUPPLY
Ten Babies Have Died in Twenty-One Days

When Mackenzie had spotted the headline in a newspaper lying on the *Phoenix* counter, a picture of a baby's coffin had risen like an unwelcome ghost in his mind.

"Father!" he'd cried without looking up, his eyes speeding through the article. "This is what's wrong with Nellie."

Frowning, Mackenzie's father had reached for his own copy of the newspaper. "Well," he'd said, "perhaps..."

Mackenzie hadn't waited. The *Phoenix* door had slapped shut behind him before his father could continue.

An astonishing jump has been made in the infant mortality statistics this month, for no less than ten babies have died inside twenty-one days of cholera infantum or summer complaint.

According to Dr. McKay, this shows an alarming condition of affairs as far as the purity of the milk supply is concerned.

Nearing the bridge, Mackenzie wove between buggies and automobiles like a marathoner passing slower runners and dashed onto the walkway.

"Excuse me," he cried, pushing between the full skirts of two women walking side by side toward him.

"Excuse me," as he dashed past a man walking a bicycle.

Ranging all the way from one and a half months to two years, that number of babies have been carried away in the city by the Grim Reaper and all, according to the medical health officer, by ailments which are preventable.

"These babies have died as a direct result of bad food," said Dr. McKay, "particularly bad milk. The milk has been dirty, and through the prevalence of dirt in it has become altogether bad, until it was sufficient to upset the tender stomach of the child."

At the end of the bridge, Mackenzie slowed, sucking in gulps of air. He squeezed the rolled-up news-paper in his fist. Then, like Tom Longboat, he tore up the Short Hill.

Every Tuesday and Friday, Mackenzie knew, a tired horse plodded down their street hauling a yellow-and-blue Smith's Dairy milk wagon. At the beginning of the block, the driver got off the wagon carrying a full basket of glass milk bottles and paper-wrapped squares of butter. Walking from door to door, he left the full bottles, picked up the empties, and from time to time called to his horse to keep up. In Mackenzie's house the two bottles of milk were fed to Nellie.

"This milk has been either dirty in the beginning through the carelessness of the man who delivered it, or kept in a dirty can or dish and in a place where the temperature was too high.

"Milk contains a certain amount of dirt anyway, and when it is kept in too warm a room, the high temperature allows the germs in the milk to hatch and multiply and accordingly the milk becomes bad, and in reality poisonous, when taken into the stomach of the child."

Cresting the hill onto Victoria Avenue, Mackenzie sped by a crew of men shovelling dirt into the trench to cover the finished water lines. He skirted the workers laying the latest pipe. Beyond Douglas Hardware, he loped past the steam engine digging out the newest part of the ditch. Without a sideways glance, he ignored the carpenters' rapping hammers and churning saws calling from the partly-built houses. Lurching on legs fast turning to rubber, he wheeled onto his street and staggered to the finish line.

"One hour. Eighteen minutes. Ten seconds," Mackenzie panted. "Seven minutes faster than the old record."

Bursting into the kitchen, he shouted, "Don't give her any milk!"

Slumped onto her mother's chest in the rocking chair, Nellie started, cried out, and whimpered. His mother shot Mackenzie an angry look. "Shush!" she said.

Mackenzie picked up Nellie's full bottle from the cool stove-top. "Did she drink any?" he gasped.

"No," his mother said. "She won't touch it."

"Good girl." Mackenzie cupped his fingers under his sister's chin. "Read this, Mother," he said, pointing to the headline, then collapsing into a chair.

"In the past week we have conducted tests on the milk produced by every dairy operating within the city of Saskatoon," Dr. McKay said, "and in many instances found evidence of impurities and germs. The following businesses distributed bad milk in that time period: City Dairy, Winnipeg Milk and Milk Products, Smith's Dairy, Robinson's Dairy.

"The best way to prevent such bad milk is to pasteurize every drop that comes into the house. This is really a very easy thing to do and will render the milk as safe as possible. The correct manner in which to pasteurize milk is to first raise its temperature ..."

Hoisting himself onto his feet, Mackenzie lifted the string and good luck penny from around his neck. He swung it like a clock's pendulum in front of Nellie. His sister ignored him. Mackenzie laid the necklace on the tray of her high chair. He reached into the woodbox and scrabbled together a handful of kindling.

A stream of tiny, sparkling stones

FROM WHERE THE BOYS SAT on the other side of the street, the boardwalk in front of the Willet looked as busy as the platform at the C.N. Station. Men stood together or sat on the edge of the planks, talking and sharing a cigarette. Others came and went from the rooming house. A small group walked slowly north toward the open field where the circus wagons would gather after they'd rolled off their special train.

"I don't want to miss seeing the elephants put up the tents this afternoon," Mackenzie said. "Let's wait and do this tomorrow. It looks like it could rain, anyway."

"We're already here," Albert said. "We'll give it five more minutes. See, those men are all leaving now. Galicians are like sheep. As soon as one does something, they all follow."

"Do you really believe that?"

"What?"

"That Galicians are like sheep."

"You don't have to believe it," Albert said. "It's just something you say."

"They're persons," Mackenzie said, "no different than you or me. And you should treat them as such."

Narrowing his eyes, Albert stared at Mackenzie. "You sound like my mother," he said.

A black horse sauntered down the street.

"Badger Breath and Four Eyes," Albert muttered as the two girls rode toward them, Eunice in the saddle and Ruth Anne holding on behind her. Albert picked up a stone. "I should nail them."

The girls didn't look their way, and when they had passed, Albert and Mackenzie headed to the Willet. Pushing his cap into his pants pocket, Mackenzie said, "You go first."

Albert flopped onto his stomach and caterpillared under the boardwalk. Before Mackenzie could follow, he caught a glimpse of the boy from Lee's Laundry bustling along the opposite side of the street. He ducked into the hollow.

"I'll head toward the barbershop," Albert said. "You take the Willet."

Within a few feet, Mackenzie found a penny, and nearby an old half-penny. He kept on until close to the Willet he spied a purple velvet bag about the size of his fist and tied with a braided golden cord. He plucked up the bag with his fingertips, laid it in the palm of his hand, and squeezed. A mound of tiny pebbles shifted in his grip. Mackenzie untied the knot and tugged at the bag's opening.

"Albert! Al-bert! Come here."

"What is it?"

"Just come here."

Albert waggled alongside Mackenzie.

"What –"

"Ssshh!" Mackenzie warned.

Heavy footsteps passed over them. The door to the rooming house opened and slapped shut.

Mackenzie held out his hand.

"Take a look," he said.

Albert exhaled. "Pay dirt!" he said. "How much is in there?"

"I don't know."

"Put your hands together."

Albert tipped the bag and jiggled it gently to release a stream of tiny, sparkling stones and five rings. "This is it, Mack," he said. "You're looking at your first fortune right in front of you." With the tip of his finger he spread the diamonds and rings across Mackenzie's palms.

"Do you think they're from Syman's?"

"How could you tell? A diamond is a diamond."

"How much do you think they're worth?"

"Plenty."

"I want to put them back in the bag," Mackenzie said. "I'm afraid of dropping some. Hold it open. Boy, oh, boy! I could buy a snap of a knife with this."

"You could buy about one thousand knives with this."

"I don't need a thousand! Only one. And anyway –"

Two pairs of boots scuffed along the boardwalk, then stopped.

"I didn't forget where it was," one man said, his shadow darkening the glitter in Mackenzie's hands. "This one plank's broken, see. So you just have to pull up the end and drop her in."

"Quick!" Mackenzie whispered." Let me pour them."

The man grunted and knelt down. The last diamonds dribbled into the bag as a man's eye blinked through the crack above Mackenzie.

"What the blazes! Get a load of this."

"What?"

"There's someone under there. No. There's two of them."

"Let me see."

Mackenzie knew who the voices belonged to. He could picture the grey cap and the shiny black hat. It was the bowler's owner who was on his knees peering at them now.

"Well, well, well," the man said. "And just look who it is, Lester. That little younker I caught snooping in the alley. He can't seem to mind his own fool business. And the other one's no better, I see. He's got our bag snatched up in his fat little fist."

"They're a couple of thieving magpies, Ezra, that's what they are," Lester said. "Can't keep their beaks off our loot."

"Snakes is more like it," Ezra said. "Their type likes to sneak around in dark holes. You see, Lester, this is why you don't put all your eggs in one nest. Some egg-sucking snake comes along and you could lose everything." He chuckled. "But not this time. No siree. I knew from the first time I laid eyes on him that boy was no good." He pushed himself up from the boardwalk.

Lester did the same. "What are we going to do with them?" he asked.

"I'm thinking," Ezra said. "How did they get in...?" He stepped onto the ground. "Here's their rabbit hole, right here. The little runts are small enough they can crawl right under." He kicked the ground to send a spray of dirt rattling onto the boardwalk. "Come over here," Ezra said. "Stand right by this hole. I'm going to take a little look-see behind the Willet. There's a pile of rubble that might come in handy. If they try to get out, you do whatever you like to stop them."

"With pleasure." Lester cackled as Ezra's footsteps tramped away.

"You can't keep us in here!" Albert shouted. "Let us out. I'm telling my pa." Nudging Mackenzie, he said, "Go. You're the closest."

"That's right, lads. Come on out. I have a little something for you." Lester slapped his fist into his palm.

Albert gave Mackenzie another push.

"I'm not moving," Mackenzie whispered.

"How are those rats keeping, Lester?" Ezra asked, his voice near again.

"I think I can reach them," Lester said. "Let me drag them out."

"No. They deserve to rot in there for awhile."

A heavy rock thumped into the dirt. Then another.

"These'll do just fine," Ezra said. "Go get more of them from that pile. There're boards, too. Grab a few of them. These vermin won't be going anywhere soon." He leaned down. "Comfy in there?"

"You have to let us go," Albert said. "It's against the law to keep us in here. My pa –"

"Shut up!" Ezra said. "You'll get out. But only after you've had a little lesson about rats messing in other people's business. Lester, put those good and snug against the side of the boardwalk." The boys felt two big stones hit the ground. "Another armful should do it."

"Help!" Albert called out. "Someone help us!"

Ezra laughed. "Don't get yourself all tied in a knot, younker," he said. "There's no one for a half-mile in any direction. They've all gone to see the circus get set up. Which is where I'm going promptly."

"What about me?" Lester asked.

"You stay here. Make sure these thieving brats don't get out of their hollow. I want them around when I get back. I won't be gone long. You can come and look around the circus with me tonight." Ezra hawked some spit. "You hear that, younkers? This is what'll be left when I'm finished with you."

Mackenzie heard the gob strike the board above

him, then felt the foul-smelling tobacco juice drip onto the back of his neck.

"My pa won't stand for this," Albert said.

MACKENZIE AND ALBERT could hear Lester mumbling to himself nearby. Every few minutes he moaned, spit, and shifted along the boardwalk.

"I knew we should have waited until tomorrow," Mackenzie whispered.

"How was I supposed to know? It was just bad luck that they came when we were here."

"I missed the circus too."

"You didn't miss the circus." Albert kept his voice low. "Just putting up the tents. The circus isn't until tomorrow."

"My mother will tan my hide for being so late getting home."

"It won't be that late. And you had your chance to get out. We could have easily outrun them."

"You can't outrun someone when you're dead."

"You wouldn't be dead. We're faster than either of them. I've been thinking what we can do when that Ezra gets back."

Outside, grey clouds darkened the sky, chilling the air and setting Lester to mutter his complaints more loudly. Thunder rolled across the railway tracks from the west. Soon shards of lightning tore through the black, letting loose a torrent of frigid rain.

Lester swore and kicked the edge of the boardwalk. "That's it," he barked. "I'm not about to ruin my health on account of you two brainless brats. That hole's stuck up tighter than a corked bottle. You're going nowhere, believe me. Unless you float away in the muck. Me, I'm off for a little refreshment."

The man's footsteps squelched away as more rain battered the planks. Streams of water spilled through the cracks and dripped like melting icicles across the boys' backs. For a long time Mackenzie and Albert wallowed in cold, dark mud.

With a grunt, someone rolled a rock away from the side of the boardwalk. A few moments later another one splashed into a puddle.

"Who's that?" Mackenzie called.

"Get ready," Albert whispered.

Mud sucked against a board as it was pried off. Cold air rushed over the boys' wet clothes. The person outside groaned, straining to lift a heavy weight. Then, "Okay," a voice said.

Mackenzie edged toward the hole. Everything outside was shades of black, even the spattered surface of the puddles.

"Go!" Albert poked Mackenzie.

"What if it's a trick?"

"There's no trick. Get going before that crook comes back."

Mackenzie pulled himself through a slough of mud in the bottom of the gully.

Albert slid out beside him. Together they peered into the dark. "Where'd he go?" Mackenzie wondered. "Who was it?"

"Don't know," Albert said, keeping his eye on the front of the Willet. "But I'm freezing. I'm going home."

The boys trudged over slippery planks to the end of the block. Mackenzie stopped short. "Dash it!" he said. "We forgot the diamonds."

Patting a bulge in his pants pocket, Albert said, "No we didn't."

Nellie's hands lay across her chest

CARRYING HIS SODDEN BOOTS, Mackenzie sloshed into the kitchen, dripping wet, muddy, and hours late for supper.

"Where have you been?" his mother cried. "Look at you! Oh! Mackenzie, what have you done to your cap? How could you possibly get it that soiled? What in heaven's name have you been doing all this time? I'm a nervous wreck. First your sister and then you! Don't take another step. Back you go and get yourself out of those clothes. Right now."

Mackenzie slunk back to the door. "We found the missing diamonds," he said to his father. "And then those men caught us."

Immediately his father was taken in by his tale. After quizzing Mackenzie, he pulled on his raincoat and rubber boots and left for the police station.

Mackenzie changed into dry clothes and slumped into his place at the table. Poking at the cold meal with his fork, he speared pale green canned peas and nibbled shreds of potato. His mother paced across the kitchen, arms pinched angrily over her chest.

"Why on earth would you want to go crawling in the mud under boardwalks?"

"It wasn't muddy until it rained."

"In the dirt, then. You've done that before, haven't you? That's how you've been getting your clothes so filthy. Don't think I haven't noticed, Mackenzie. I'm the one doing your laundry. If little Nell hadn't been so sick, I might've put a stop to it."

"But we got the diamonds for Mr. Syman. Those robbers would have sold them."

"You should leave diamonds and robbers to the police. What might have happened if those wretched men had come back? Surely they were planning on hurting you."

"Father says they were probably just trying to scare us."

"Why would they stop at scaring you? They could just as easily beat you. You would have been helpless."

"We were going to get away as soon as we were out. We could easily outrun them."

Closing her eyes, his mother sighed. "Enough," she said. "Enough."

Mackenzie pushed away from the table.

"Off to bed with you," his mother said. "I'll talk to you in the morning."

It wasn't until he was under the covers and about to blow out his light that it struck Mackenzie. For the first time in days, Nellie had not been slumped whimpering in Mother's arms. He swung his feet onto the floor and tiptoed into his sister's room. In the grey light he could see Nellie lying on her back, her hands overlapped on her chest. Like that baby in the coffin, Mackenzie thought, trembling. He leaned over so his face was about a foot above the bed, held his breath, and listened. The thump-thump of his own heart filled his ears.

"Nellie," he whispered. She didn't stir.

Pursing his lips, he blew a stream of breath over his sister's face, ruffling the hair fallen onto the pillow. She didn't twitch.

Leaning further over, Mackenzie touched his nose to her forehead. His sister's warm breath tickled his lips. Exhaling, he kissed the tip of her nose. As he straightened up, a dull glint on Nellie's chest caught his eye. Gently lifting her hands, Mackenzie spied the flattened penny clutched tightly in her fingers.

Back in his room, he quietly slid open the top drawer of his dresser. Reaching inside, he lifted out a small box and a five-inch piece of peeled stick. Mackenzie climbed under the covers, sat up against the wall at the head of his bed, dimmed the wick on his lamp, and set to work.

The Daily Phoenix

FRIDAY JULY 16, 1912

CIRCUS PERFORMERS WILL PITCH THEIR CAMP

A. G. Barnes Gives Parade and Performances Tomorrow

Tomorrow is circus day and once again the small child is joyful with the thoughts of what he will see and hear when he enters the Big Tent. The A. G. Barnes' wagons will arrive on the train today and be driven to the showgrounds where the Layout Man will decide the location for each piece of canvas and length of pole. Boys young and old who gather to watch will delight in the no-nonsense directions given to circus roustabouts and trained riggers as well as local rubes who hope to receive a free pass for their efforts.

Mammoth tents will nose their way into the air as if by magic as the towering center poles are pulled easily into place by agreeable elephants who, no doubt, will welcome the opportunity to stretch their legs after their recent journey.

The first part of the circus program tomorrow will be the street parade, preceded as always by a hearty crier who will hail the traditional warning, "Hang onto your horses, the elephants are coming!" Led by four trumpeting military bands, the pageant of the A. G. Barnes circus will leave the showgrounds at 9:30 o'clock.

It has been confirmed that a steam-driven calliope will be the last carriage in the grand parade. This portable pipe organ is sure to draw people like a pied piper to the showgrounds where the first performance begins at one o'clock.

CHAPTER EIGHT
Saturday, July 17, 1912

What knife did you use?

MACKENZIE WATCHED THE PUDDLE OF molasses slowly melt and seep into the porridge he'd found on the warming shelf above the range. When only a thin brown pool remained on top, he picked up his spoon and churned the mound. Licking off the molasses, he was reminded that it didn't taste as good as his favourite topping, butter. But his mother, he knew, had buried every bit of their butter in her garden after reading about the unclean dairies. Wolfishly, he attacked the porridge. He was late getting out of bed and Mackenzie's spoon click-clicked against the side of his bowl in an empty kitchen.

He was standing at the wash basin on the counter when his mother came inside carrying Nellie. His sister was sitting up straight, her bare arms pushing against his mother's chest.

"Hi, Nellie," he said.

His sister twisted round, held out her arms, and cried, "Mack!"

Sitting at a chair, Mackenzie reached up to take her. "How is she?" he asked.

"Her fever's going down and she's eating again. Dr. Weaver was here earlier to take a look at her. He says it's too early to tell if she's over it."

"What did she have?"

Mackenzie's mother shrugged. "He doesn't know. I guess the important thing is that's she's getting better."

"Do you like your lucky penny, Nellie?" Mackenzie said, flipping his finger under the coin hanging from his sister's neck.

"She won't take it off," his mother said. "Even when I gave her a little bath this morning."

Nellie wrapped her fingers around Mackenzie's nose and squeezed. "Ow!" he cried and rubbed his thumbs in her armpits. She squirmed, released her hand, and screamed.

"Your father would like you to go to his office right away." Seeing Mackenzie's frown, his mother continued, "The police want to talk to you about everything that happened. Albert, too."

"What about the parade? I don't want to miss it."

"If you hurry maybe," his mother said, sweeping a few loose strands of hair behind her ear.

Mackenzie lifted his sister's arms until she stood up and pumped her legs on his thighs. He took both her hands in one of his and reached into his pants pocket. "Look, Nellie, this is for you," he said. His sister grabbed the stick, studied it closely, then sat down on Mackenzie's legs. Chewing an end of the toy, she traced the grooves with her fingertips.

"What's that you've given her?"

"A toy," Mackenzie said. "I made it."

"How nice," his mother said. "Thank you." She walked closer. "From that stick? Did you use one of my knives after I told you not to?"

"No."

"What knife did you use?"

"I borrowed one."

"Well, you did a very good job." She turned back to the counter. Lifting up a small glass bottle, she asked, "Do you know anything about this? I found it on the doorstep this morning."

Mackenzie shifted his sister onto his shoulder and stood up. Taking the bottle from his mother, he read the words hand-printed on the glued-on label. "One half spoon for a baby." He undid the cap and sniffed the dark brown liquid. "Ou," he said, wrinkling his nose. "I think Stanley brought this." He explained what his friend had said.

"I'm not sure what to do with it."

"Keep it," Mackenzie said. "In case we need it another time." After a moment, he asked, "When are we going to get water?"

"Soon. Your father and I talked about it again last

night. I don't think I could live through another scare with Nellie." His mother held out her arms. "I'll take her," she said. "How be you leave your chores for now and go do your business with your father. And have fun at the circus. I don't think Nellie's ready for that yet. I'll take her down to Cairns to look at their petticoats. I'd like her to have a new one for church tomorrow."

WHEN MACKENZIE SLIPPED THROUGH the open doorway, he heard Mr. Douglas talking to someone in the back room. The boxes of knives were inside the display case. He slid his hand into his pocket, rested his fingertips on top of the cabinet, and heard a soft chunk as the box dropped onto the glass. After gently snugging down his cap, Mackenzie strolled toward the door.

The sergeant can wait

MACKENZIE AND HIS FATHER hiked down Third Avenue.

"The part that baffles me," his father said, "is who let you out last night."

"Me too. He just showed up, whoever it was."

"Sergeant Devereux will probably ask you about that. And anything you can tell him about those crooks."

"I only saw them through the cracks. But I know

who they are. They're the same ones I told you about, the pickpockets at the station. Dad, do you think we'll get the reward? We found the missing jewellery."

"We'll see what the sergeant says."

"If I got half of the money, would that be enough to get water for our house?"

"I don't think we should count on anything yet." Mackenzie's father slowed to look past some hoarding into the excavation across the back alley from Flanagan's Hotel. "Look, they've got the cement mixer set up." He pointed to a large, round steel tub as big as a boxcar that sat at the edge of the hole. A loop of thick leather belt connected the machine to an idle steam engine. "They'll fire it up on Monday. Once they start the walls, it will begin to look like a real building."

"I can hear the calliope," Mackenzie said, as a windy tune that sounded like a giant's stuttering whistle floated down the street.

"'My Merry Oldsmobile.'"

"It sounds close."

"*Come away with me, Lucille,*" Mackenzie's father sang along. "*In my Merry Oldsmobile. Down the road of life we'll fly ...*" He pulled out his watch. "It's after eleven," he said. "They'll be heading back to the circus grounds."

"I missed the parade?"

Snapping his watch closed, his father said, "I suppose the sergeant can wait a bit longer. If we hurry, we might catch the tail end."

THE ELEPHANTS HAD LUMBERED down the street and around the corner before Mackenzie and his father arrived. They heard the last two marching bands and saw at least a dozen horse-drawn wagons, each brightly painted with the name and colours of the circus. The tops of the side walls had been removed from the wagons to show windows protected with heavy bars. At times, through the bars, the head of a lion or a tiger could be seen looking back at the crowds staring its way.

A team of six white horses pulled the bright blue-and-yellow calliope wagon at the end of the procession. A driver perched high on top of the wagon. Under him, seen through a small window, sat the tired, heavily-perspiring organ player. The calliope's brass pipes were visible through a middle window. At the back, extra-large wheels, the size of a locomotive's, carried the steam engine, the engineer, and his helper. A small wagon hitched to the rear of the calliope carried the last of the engine's wood supply.

Plumes of white steam shot up from the pipes as the whistles blasted a tune. Young children sitting on the curbs cried out and threw their hands over their ears.

"'The Old Grey Mare,'" Mackenzie's father shouted. "Like your mother plays." As the calliope rolled further down the street, he nodded his head for Mackenzie to follow. "They say you can hear those whistles ten miles out in the country." He chuckled.

"I wager the further away you are, the better it sounds." Reaching into his jacket pocket, he showed Mackenzie four red tickets.

"One for you," he said. "One for me. And two extras. Mr. Aikin always gives a free ticket to each of the boys who deliver the papers. These are leftovers. You'll still have time to find someone after you've spoken to Sergeant Devereux."

Give my swamper a hand

ONE HOUR LATER Mackenzie was walking down Twentieth Street toward First Avenue when he recognized Blackie and Star hitched to a newly painted dray in front of the Queens Hotel. Henry Lavallée sat on the seat, his blue beret snugged on his head, towering above a man speaking to him from the sidewalk. A wide strip of white cloth that looked like a folded bed-sheet was wrapped around Henry Lavallée's middle, pinning his left arm to his chest.

Mackenzie crossed the street to stand in front of the horses. He rubbed their foreheads and in return was knocked onto his heels when Blackie's powerful head butted against his chest.

Glancing past the team, Mackenzie saw that it was Ichabod Crane talking to Henry Lavallée. Ichabod glanced toward Mackenzie, tipped his straw boater to Henry Lavallée, and walked away. Stepping onto the sidewalk, Mackenzie ran his hand along Star's thick shoulders and flank.

Looking up at Henry Lavallée, he asked, "Did you hurt your arm?"

"I did," Henry Lavallée said. "And the doctor told me I have to be careful."

"You can't lift things?"

Raising his right hand, Henry Lavallée said, "I can still lift more with this one arm than other men can with two. What is hard for me is to climb up and down from my wagon many times every day." He slapped the other side of the seat. "Now I have a swamper. He can jump on and off and carry in the smaller loads. Sometimes he helps me balance the big ones. There are still two boxes to take in. Why don't you give him a hand?"

Turning to the back of the wagon, Mackenzie found himself face to face with Stanley.

"I'm supposed to help the swamper," Mackenzie said, looking past his friend.

"I am the swamper," Stanley said.

"You are? When did that happen?"

"This morning."

"These two gentlemen," Henry Lavallée cut in, shaking the reins, "are not used to standing about so long."

"I will be right back," Stanley called. To Mackenzie he said, "We have to take them in to the desk." He dragged two boxes to the back edge of the dray.

Hefting one on his shoulder, he left the second for Mackenzie. The two boys walked into the dark lobby of the Queens Hotel and heaved the boxes onto a counter.

"I had to show Henry Lavallée that I was strong enough," Stanley said, grinning. "And I had to wait for him to talk to my mother."

"And she said, 'yes'? What about school?"

"Maybe I will go back. Maybe I will not. We will talk at the end of the summer."

"I found the diamonds," Mackenzie said, "from Syman's store. Albert and I did. They were under a boardwalk."

"You will get the reward. Seventy-five dollars."

"No. The jewels we found were only part of what was stolen. But Mr. Syman gave us ten dollars to share. My father's keeping my half for me." The boys started back to the door. "You were there, weren't you?" Mackenzie asked. "At Syman's?"

Stanley nodded. "I went there before the car crashed. Then I ran away." He laughed. "But I did not steal any jewels."

"What were you doing?"

Stanley lowered his voice. "My mother asked me to sell her rings."

"What rings?"

"Her wedding ring and other ones her family had given her. We needed the money."

"Did you sell them?"

"No," Stanley said. "The automobile came through the window before I could talk to Mr. Syman."

"So why did you run away? You didn't do anything wrong."

"The police," Stanley said. "Maybe for you they will say you did not do anything wrong. But for a Galician they would."

"What do you mean?"

"Already some people say that my mother cannot take care of five children by herself. They want to take away my sisters. If the police knew why I was there ..." Stanley shrugged.

"But then Mr. Lavallée asked me to be his swamper. So we don't have to sell the rings, anyway." He pushed through the door.

Stanley climbed onto the wagon, squeezed in beside Henry Lavallée, and took the reins.

Calling, "Giyup! Giyup, boys!" Stanley slapped the leather along the horses' backs.

Blackie swung his head around and fixed Stanley with one eye.

"Giyup!" Stanley cried. Star whinnied, but neither horse moved.

Henry Lavallée slapped his knee. "Enough! Let's get this rig rolling." The wagon jerked forward and rolled onto First Avenue.

Mackenzie waved to Stanley, then slipped off his cap. Frowning, he rubbed his hand over a smear of dried mud. He spit on the stain and pulled his thumbnail over the cloth. With a sigh he put the soiled cap back on. Sliding his hand into his pants pocket, he pinched the two tickets between his fingers. It was too late to find some friends to take to the circus, he decided.

Free tickets, you go

THE CHINESE BOY strolled toward Mackenzie, the empty green bags bouncing lightly from the ends of his long pole. Pulling the tickets from his pocket, Mackenzie stepped in front of the boy.

"Circus!" he said. "Lions! Tigers!" He paused. "Roar!"

The boy glanced at Mackenzie, then stared straight ahead.

"Big tent!" Beginning to feel foolish, Mackenzie held his arms over his head. "Elephants!" He rested his cheek on his shoulder and held his arm in front of his body.

When the Chinese boy shook his head, Mackenzie thrust the tickets at his chest. "Free tickets," he said. "You go."

Swinging his pole to the side, the boy began to walk away.

"No!" Mackenzie cried, raising his voice. "Wait. Tickee! Tickee! You go! Free! No pay!"

The boy reached out, pushed Mackenzie's arm to the side, and strode past. Mackenzie watched him as far as Lee's Laundry where he left the sidewalk to walk along the side of the building to the back.

When Mackenzie entered the laundry, Mr. Lee looked up from his ironing table and smiled.

"No shirts today," he said. "Nothing for Mr. Davis."

"I know," Mackenzie said. He held up two slips of red paper. "I have these."

When Mr. Lee came closer, Mackenzie laid them on the counter.

"The circus," Mackenzie said. "These are free tickets. For the boy who works here."

Shaking his head, Mr. Lee said, "Not here."

"I know," Mackenzie said. "I just saw him. I'm leaving these for him."

"There is no boy here," Mr. Lee repeated.

Mackenzie felt tired. He patted the tickets. "For you, then," he said.

Mr. Lee began to say something, but Mackenzie raised his hands and backed away. "No," he said. "You keep them." Fleeing out the door, he heard Mr. Lee call, "Okay!"

Get your program!

TWO POLES TOWERED high above the earth to the distant peaks of the white canvas tent. Mackenzie spied the small aerialists' platform on each pole and the tightrope strung between. On the ground below, three rings made of curved wood painted red had fresh sawdust inside. Mackenzie turned his gaze to the blue curtain draped over a rope that hung across one end of the big tent. The performers would appear from behind that curtain, he knew.

Hundreds of people milled about near the rings or, like Mackenzie and his father, climbed into the bleachers to claim their seats. Here rows of other posts, shorter than the centre poles but still as high as a house, held up the roof and walls that surrounded them.

"We forgot to buy a program," Mackenzie's father shouted above the swirling voices. Pressing two coins into Mackenzie's palm, he added, "Get yourself some popcorn while you're there." He pulled his notebook from his jacket pocket. "I'm going to talk to a few people."

"What about?"

Waving his arm slowly around the tent, Mackenzie's father said, "All this." The skin around his eyes crinkled. "The circus."

"I'll be right back." Mackenzie scrambled past the people seated in his row, then squirmed around those coming up the steps. First he bought a bag of popcorn, then he joined a line waiting to get a program.

"Five cents," he heard the seller call. "Get your program. Five cents. All about the biggest circus."

One by one Mackenzie picked puffy, white kernels from the top of the bag. When it was his turn, he held out a nickel to the program seller. It was John.

"Five cents," the older boy said, taking the coin,

dropping it into the cloth pouch around his waist, and handing over a folded paper.

"Why are you selling programs?" Mackenzie asked. "What about the boys who work for you?"

"Not one," John said, wagging a finger at Mackenzie, "Not one would do this job. All they cared for was to see the show. I tell you, you'll get nowhere in this life if all you want is to sit and watch the world go by." He reached over Mackenzie's shoulder then dropped another coin into his pouch. "Programs here," he cried. Mackenzie rolled up the paper and shoved it into his pants pocket.

Tell us what you did with our loot

RETURNING TO THE STANDS with the bag of popcorn held against his chest, Mackenzie spied a familiar grey cap, then the black bowler. The men were walking away from him, toward the rings. Mackenzie veered into the crowd to get closer. The two thieves squeezed a third man between them, their hands flicking into the man's pockets before they released him. Mackenzie kept pace with the crooks. Two girls stood a few feet away with their backs to them. It was Badger Breath and Four Eyes, talking to each other and sometimes glancing up into the stands. Each carried a straw bag hooked to her elbow.

Could it have been them, Mackenzie wondered, who let us out last night? They might have seen us crawling under, or ridden back when those men were blocking the hole.

Mackenzie spotted a police constable in a tall blue helmet walking into the throng about twenty feet in front of the pickpockets. Instantly the black bowler changed direction, pulling the grey cap in his wake. They were headed toward the girls.

Gripping his popcorn, Mackenzie rushed after them. The girls' bags, he could see, were open at their sides. The black bowler held his hand in front of him, ready to pounce. Mackenzie was close enough now that if he yelled the girls might turn around in time to foil the pickpockets. Would Badger Breath and Four Eyes have gone through the rain and the dark and the mud to save him?

Mackenzie darted around the last adult in his path. Lowering his shoulder like a charging rugby player he knocked into Badger Breath, toppling her and Four Eyes onto the dusty ground.

"Ooh. Sorry," Mackenzie said when the girls rolled over to face their attacker.

"You moron," Eunice fumed as she struggled to her feet. "You stupid oaf!" She brushed her hand over her dress.

Mackenzie stepped away from the girls and checked over his shoulder to where the pickpockets had been. They were gone. Twisting sideways, he worked his way toward the police constable. The officer was bending his head, nodding at a woman jabbing a finger toward his chest.

"I found my handbag!" Mackenzie heard the woman shout as he got closer. "The thief dropped it after he removed my change purse. It's terribly dirty of course but it isn't damaged."

"Did you see the culprit, ma'am?"

"No. He came up behind me in the crush. The first thing I knew, he ripped my bag from my hand. By the time I got turned around he'd disappeared into this mob. How can you let people like that run loose? A woman should feel safe. Is this what your city has become? A haven for thieves and robbers?"

"There's quite an assembly here today, ma'am," the constable said, straightening up and studying the crowd over the woman's head. "Quite an assembly. We can't be looking everywhere at once." He nodded slightly and touched his fingers to his helmet to tell the woman her interview was over.

Mackenzie shouldered his way to the officer. "I saw some pickpockets," he said. "They were stealing things from people all around them."

"Aye, lad," the constable said, glancing briefly down at Mackenzie. "That's what they do, those pickpockets."

"One's wearing a grey cap and the other one has a black bowler, sort of scuffed and shiny. They were right over there." Mackenzie pointed.

"Where are they now, boy, these robbers you saw? I can see any number of men who match that description."

"I don't know where they went. But they were here."

"You let me know when you spot them, lad. For now I suggest that you find your seat. The show will be starting soon." The constable touched his fingers to his helmet and walked away.

More people were leaving the floor of the tent and peering into the bleachers to find the remaining seats. Mackenzie spotted the boy from the laundry and Mr. Lee shuffling down a row and squeezing into the last empty space. Smiling, the boy studied the three wooden rings, glanced high up to the top of the tent, and let his eyes sweep over the crowd. He looked toward Mackenzie, then quickly past him as the blue curtain parted and the Ringmaster stepped through. Setting his megaphone on the ground, the man twisted the tips of his waxed moustache, and rubbed his palms together.

Mackenzie opened the popcorn bag and plucked out three kernels. He scanned the crowd around him. The black bowler and grey cap were nowhere to be seen. He turned back. A mass of people as big as the horde in front of the Cairns Store waited to climb into the stands between him and his seat. Scurrying to the back of the bleachers nearest the blue curtain, he stepped into the shadowy maze of timbers that supported the stands. He smiled at the sight of the dozens of backsides on the planks above him. Albert should be here, he thought. Lots of coins must fall from these people's pockets. Bending down, he twisted under and around the boards as he worked his way toward his father.

Finding himself in a small open space Mackenzie stood up to get his bearings. A hand swung out of the darkness behind him and clamped onto his shoulder.

"What are you up to now, younker?" a voice growled.

Mackenzie knew who it was.

Pinching his fingernails into Mackenzie's skin, Ezra said, "You looking for that beating you missed?" A wad of tobacco flew past Mackenzie, spraying brown spit onto his cheek. A rough hand clamped over his mouth. "Don't think about making any noise," Ezra hissed. "No one's going to hear you. Not a one. All they care about right now is what's going on in the circus."

"Let him go!" a voice cried. "I'll tell the police."

"Who let you in?" Lester sneered, sidling into the opening. "I thought you'd know by now people don't want the likes of you around here."

"I'll tell the police," the voice repeated.

Mackenzie tried to twist around, but Ezra's fingers tightened on his shoulder and mouth.

"Now just what," Lester snarled, "would a little black-haired cur like you want to tell the police?"

"I don't care what you call me. I saw you last night. You trapped the boys under the sidewalk."

"Grab him," Ezra growled. "He's one more brat who needs a good beating. And you," Ezra shook Mackenzie, "are going to tell us what you did with our loot."

"Now what loot would that be, Ezra?"

Sergeant Devereux! Mackenzie recognized his voice.

"Don't think about running off, Ezra," the sergeant said, bending down and stepping toward Lester. Straightening up, the sergeant rested his hands on his hips. He was taller than Ezra, and heavier, and wore his peaked cap low on his forehead. "Let the young lad go."

Mackenzie felt Ezra's hands drop away. "I've got nothing to say to you," the robber spat.

"Maybe not now," Sergeant Devereux said. "You may change your mind. I've got a feeling you're going to be spending a lot of time with us, Ezra." He smiled at Mackenzie. "Thank you lads," he said. "I know where to find you if I need you. You'd better scoot now or you'll miss the show."

Mackenzie looked around. The Chinese boy was a few feet away, waving at him to follow. Behind him a police constable stood with his arms crossed over his chest, staring hard at Lester.

"Were you just talking in English?" Mackenzie asked. "Did you say you saw us last night? Was it you who rescued us?"

The boy didn't answer. With a last wave at Mackenzie he turned and hurried along the back of the stands.

"Wait!" Mackenzie called. Then he rushed to try and catch up.

The boy swung into a passageway between two sets of bleachers as a trumpet sounded from the centre of the tent. "Ta-da-da-dat-ta-da!" The Ringmaster's voice called out, "Ladies and Gentlemen! Please find your seats. We are about to begin."

The noise of the crowd lessened. The Chinese boy left the passageway and walked along the front of the bleachers. Mackenzie joined him.

"So you speak English," Mackenzie said. "That's why you understand everything. But was it you who let us out?"

The boy nodded. He stopped and half-turned to the stands. "My seat is up here," he said, "with my uncle."

"Mine's further down, with my father. Thank you for rescuing us."

The Chinese boy stepped onto the bleacher stairs. A few moments later Mackenzie was squeezing down the row toward his seat. His father was gone. Mackenzie sat down on the plank. Almost immediately Albert dropped down beside him, elbowing Mackenzie in the ribs. He wore a grey plaid suit with knee-high pants and a bow tie. Thrusting his fingers under his white collar, Albert rolled his eyes.

"I just saw you with that laundry boy," he said. "Since when can you speak Chinese?"

"I can't."

"What were you doing with him then?"

"He is a person," Mackenzie started to say.

"I know, I know," Albert interrupted. "No different than you or me. But what were you doing?"

"I was thanking him. He's the one who let us out from under the boardwalk last night."

"Him?"

"Yes. And he speaks English."

"He does? How can he do that?"

Mackenzie shrugged. Before he could think of an answer, his father returned. "I'm back," he said, standing beside the boys. "Just in time, I believe. Albert, I saw your parents a few rows back. They'd like you to join them."

Albert stood up. "Are you telling me the truth?" When Mackenzie nodded, Albert turned toward the steps.

"Ta-da-da-dat-ta-da!" the trumpet blew.

The big tent grew as quiet as a church when the minister says, "Let us pray." Leaning back, Mackenzie unrolled the top of the popcorn bag. The Ringmaster raised the megaphone to his lips.

"Ladies and gentlemen!" he roared. "Welcome to the A.G. Barnes Circus! The greatest wild animal performance on the western plains! Prepare yourselves to be frightened and delighted! Awed and amazed and amused! Baffled and enthralled!

"Waiting to entertain you are Captain Ricardo, Captain Stonewall, Madam Florine and hundreds of others, human and animal. A special delight will come when we introduce to you for the first time the strongest man ever to perform with our circus. A man so powerful you will think his feats humanly impossible. So astounding you must witness them here in this ring with your own eyes. A man only recently arrived in North America from his home in the shade of the mighty Alps, near the shores of the ancient Adriatic Sea. The gargantuan, the grandiose, the Great Gorgonzola!"

The audience clapped and cheered.

"Gorgonzola?" Mackenzie shouted into his father's ear. "What happened to the Mighty Marmaduke?"

"The Mighty Marmaduke lost to Henry Lavallée. So he's not the strongest on the western plains anymore."

"Now it's someone new? The Great Gorgonzola?"

Mackenzie's father nodded. "Maybe not entirely new. Let's wait until we get a look at him."

"Yes, ladies and gentlemen," the Ringmaster called, lowering his voice. "The time has finally come. Let the show begin!"

The Daily Phoenix

SATURDAY JULY 17, 1912

CITY NOW USES 2,000 GALLONS OF ICE CREAM PER DAY

Every Cooling Parlour in City Reports Record Business

The smile of Old Sol himself is no broader these days than is the smile of the ice cream and soda water men. From early morning until the cool shades that come just before midnight, he is busy smiling and dipping the cold cream from the large can, placing it before the small boy--and, especially during these warm and collar-melting days, before the small and large man--and, stacking up big piles of dimes.

The consensus of opinion is that Saskatoon is using ice cream at the rate of 2,000 gallons a day. For a small city such as Saskatoon is, this is a wonderful amount to use and indicates an ice cream appetite that simply won't behave.

The Hub Confectionery store and ice cream parlour reports the greatest sales. Over the counter it handles anywhere from sixty to eighty gallons a day with a hundred on Saturdays. At great cost, the management have just installed a continuous ice cream freezer which is able to turn out a constant stream of frozen coolness at the rate of 50 gallons an hour.

Should a mother worry that her young children might fall ill from eating our city's ice cream? Not at all, say the parlour proprietors, only the purest milks are used in the dessert's production.

Surely that is common knowledge, because in the past weeks it has been an almost impossible matter to secure a seat in any city soda fountain.

CHAPTER NINE
Monday, July 19, 1912

He'll have those scoundrels in court

MACKENZIE WATCHED HIS MOTHER LADLE scoops of creamy porridge into his bowl. "Thank you," he said, spooning on molasses. He stirred until the dark brown liquid coloured the mound of steaming oatmeal. Beside him his father drank a cup of tea. On the other side of the table, Nellie happily used her new wooden toy to push little hills of cooled porridge across her high chair tray. Mackenzie's mother refilled his father's cup, poured tea for herself, and sat down.

"Did Mr. Marmaduke look happy with his new name?" she asked.

"He never looks happy," Mackenzie said, blowing over the top of his heaping spoon. "He always looks like he doesn't know what he's going to be asked to do next."

"But he did everything they said he could," Mackenzie's father added. He turned to Mackenzie's mother. "The one I liked the best was when he hitched himself to an elephant's wagon that's usually hauled by four horses and pulled it into the middle of the tent. With the elephant inside! He did some other amazing things too. If Henry Lavallée had been there, even he would have been impressed."

"You could write a story about him," Mackenzie's mother said.

"It's too late this year, Maude. The circus has packed up and gone."

"What news are you going after?" Mackenzie asked.

"Well, first off –" Mackenzie's father stood up and drank the last of the tea from his cup. "First off, I'm going to have a chat with Sergeant Devereux. I expect he'll have those scoundrels in court this morning. We'll see what the magistrate has to say." His father took his boater from a shelf and tapped it lightly onto his head.

With one hand on the door knob, he turned to Mackenzie. "You won't forget about meeting me?"

"No!"

Mackenzie's father nodded and a moment later the door slapped shut behind him.

"May I have more please?" Mackenzie asked.

"Yes. Have all you like," his mother answered. "Your sister's already had a huge helping."

"Is she all better?" Mackenzie pushed back his

chair, walked to the range, and emptied the porridge pot into his bowl. "Do you know yet what was she sick from?"

"Mack!" Nellie cried when he walked past her on his way to the table. She slapped her hand down to flatten a mound of porridge onto the tray.

"Dr. Weaver can't tell for sure," his mother said. "It wasn't typhoid, or she wouldn't be this lively so soon. He's going to drop by this afternoon and give her a good checking over. Maybe he'll know more then." She took a sip of tea. "I'm just going to sit a minute, Mackenzie, then I'm going to get busy. I'll need your help."

Mackenzie sat down, dribbled on molasses, and started to eat. "What with?" he asked.

"It's washday. I think you dirtied every piece of clothing to your name last week. Even with what's in the cistern, we won't have enough water. You'll have to go see Mrs. Bailey with your pails." Mackenzie's mother rested her cup on her saucer. "When the reservoir is full, you can go off and see your friends. What is it you're doing with your father?"

Without looking up, Mackenzie slowly spooned the last of the porridge from his bowl.

"Does it have anything to do with that reward money you were given?"

Mackenzie nodded. "Yes," he said, grinning. "He's going to buy me a knife. I already know which one I'll choose"

The Daily Phoenix

MONDAY JULY 19, 1912

PICKPOCKETS AND PETTY THIEVES FILL POLICE CELLS

Light-Fingered Gang Taken out of Business

Chief Dunning's officers were kept busy this morning escorting a steady stream of culprits from the crowded police cells to the Magistrate's Court. Many of those arrested had been caught practising their dishonourable habits in the crowded spaces inside the tents of the A. G. Barnes Circus.

Included in this parade were two gentlemen who have been the subject of a police investigation that lasted many days. Mr. Ezra Coates and Mr. Lester Laird were charged with a host of offences that include pickpocketing passengers at the Canadian Northern Station and stealing a quantity of diamonds and other valuables last week from the shattered window of Syman's Jewellers. That these two showed up at the A.G. Barnes Circus full of intent to continue their light-fingered ways showed more greed than good judgement. Once noticed by the constables on duty in the crowd, the pair were quickly apprehended and taken out of business.

Some of the jewels stolen from Mr. Syman were discovered Friday afternoon last by two local lads in a bag under a boardwalk. Although this was only a portion of what had been taken, the storekeeper opened his till and drew out a ten spot which he offered to the boys as a token reward.

Magistrate Brown invited Mr. Coates and Mr. Laird to continue their stay in the King's jail until their trial can be held next week.

Acknowledgements

WHEN I BEGAN MY RESEARCH FOR THIS STORY, I quickly learned that there are many wonderful sources of information about the Canadian prairies in the year 1912. I read newspapers, books, and pamphlets and studied displays, artifacts, and maps and my mind filled with images of that time. As the story began to take form, and my fictional characters went about their lives, I had to decide which real people and what actual places to include.

None of the main characters – Mackenzie, his friends and family, Lester and Ezra, and Henry Lavallée – are based on real people. However, John Diefenbaker was a teenager living in Saskatoon in 1912. For a few years he organized a group of younger boys to sell newspapers for him. Later, as an adult, he many times tried and failed to win elections. Eventually, he succeeded and became the Prime Minister of Canada in 1957. Dr. W. J. McKay served tirelessly as Saskatoon's Medical Health Officer from 1906 to 1912. The editor of *The Daily Phoenix* at the time was a Mr. Aikin. Tom Longboat and Johnny Hayes were well-known long distance runners.

The *Daily Phoenix* reports that appear throughout the story are based on actual *Phoenix* articles. Each one also has been shaped by fiction.

A number of real places are mentioned. Some of them I've moved from their actual location so they would fit the story better. For example, Cairns Store, the Douglas Hardware, and Lee's Laundry really existed. So did Harry Tupling's, the Nifty Man's Store. The Willet rooming house, McMahon's Dry Goods Store, and many other places, I made up.

Numerous people helped me gather the information that I needed to write this novel. The staffs of the Local History Room of the Saskatoon Public Library, the Saskatoon branch and the Curatorial Centre of the Western Development Museum, the Special Collections Department of the University of Saskatchewan Library, the Saskatchewan Archives Board, and the City of Saskatoon Archives repeatedly located information I sought and suggested additional sources. Volunteers of the WDM, the Pion-Era show, and the Saskatchewan Railway Museum proved to be passionate and informed resources themselves. Bill Waiser, Verne Clemence, Don Kerr, Phyllis Glaze, and Alice Glaze freely shared their time and ideas. Arlene Shiplett graciously allowed me to try my hand on the WDM's calliope. Thanks to all of you. Any errors or misinterpretations of local history are my responsibility.

About the author

DAVE GLAZE is the author of the Pelly stories: *Pelly,
Waiting for Pelly,* and the upcoming *Save Pelly.* He also
wrote *Who took Henry and Mr. Z?*, a finalist in the children's category of the Arthur Ellis Crime Writers
Awards. *The Light-fingered Gang* is the first novel in his
new historical fiction series, The Mackenzie Davis Files.

Dave Glaze was born in New Westminster, British
Columbia, and grew up in towns in Alberta, Ontario,
and Saskatchewan. At various times he's made his
living as a journalist, a social worker, a landscaper, and
a lumber mill worker, but for most of his working life
he's been a teacher and teacher-librarian in elementary
schools. He has written for and helped to edit a number
of magazines. Besides working on his own writing, he
enjoys giving readings, presentations, and writing
workshops to children and adults.